THE GLASS CITY

and other stories

REVISED EDITION

THE GLASS CITY

and other stories

REVISED EDITION

JEN KNOX

Hollywood Books International
the fiction imprint of Press Americana

Published by
Hollywood Books International
the fiction imprint of Press Americana

americanpopularculture.com

Cover Art: Christopher J. Shanahan

Library of Congress Cataloging-in-Publication Data

Names: Knox, Jen, 1979- author.
Title: The glass city : and other stories / Jen Knox.
Other titles: Glass city (Compilation : 2023)
Description: Revised edition. | Hollywood : Hollywood Books
International, [2023] | Summary: "Winner of the Prize Americana
for Prose, Jen Knox's The Glass City and Other Stories is a shrewd
yet playful collection that explores the dangers of climate change
with subtle, skillful elegance. An aging acrobat looks for
connectivity online as her city floods, sisters spread their mother's
ashes on flowers that no longer exist, a reluctant host shares an
island's secrets, and families survive natural disasters that shake
out lies and destroy inhibitions"-- Provided by publisher.
Identifiers: LCCN 2023017557 | ISBN 9781735360171 (paperback)
Subjects: LCSH: Climatic changes--Fiction. | LCGFT: Ecofiction. |
    Short stories.
Classification: LCC PS3611.N693 G57 2023 | DDC 813/.6--
dc23/eng/20230414
LC record available at https://lccn.loc.gov/2023017557

for my family

CONTENTS

FOREWORD

We are on the cusp of something unimaginable. That is how wrapping our mind around the planet in global warming time often feels. Which is why, as Amitav Ghosh has famously noted, given the urgency of the crisis, it is astonishing how little of it has thus far entered our fictional worlds. In his work *The Great Derangement*, Ghosh reflects on why this is so. He argues that part of the problem is that the catastrophic and unpredictable nature of climate change seems to make a mockery of the kinds of structured plots and epiphanies and character arcs that serious fiction depends on. He explains that "in the era of global warming, nothing is really far away; there is no place where the orderly expectations of bourgeois life hold unchallenged sway. It is as though our earth had become a literary critic and were laughing at Flaubert, Chatterjee, and their like, mocking their mockery of the 'prodigious happenings' that occur so often in romances and epic poems…these are not ordinary times: the events that mark them are not easily accommodated in the deliberately prosaic world of serious prose fiction."

Yet Ghosh also argues – for me, very movingly – that neither is science fiction or magical realism entirely equipped to prepare or console or teach us how to live through this complicated time. He states, "But there is another reason why, from the writer's point of view, it would serve no purpose to approach them in that way: because to treat them as magical or surreal would be to rob them of precisely the quality that makes them so urgently compelling – which is that they are actually happening on this earth, at this time."

As I read Jen Knox's stories in *The Glass City*, this phrase from Ghosh keeps knocking around my head: "actually happening on this earth, at this time." The reason I keep repeating it under my breath is that Jen Knox has somehow managed to combine the serious attention to the real, the deep facticity of great prose fiction as we have known it, with precisely the science fiction or horror or magical elements that our time – this remarkable and terrifying age of miracles – seems to demand.

When we speak of visionary work in literature, the phrase all too often conjures up tired and/or melodramatic associations. We picture Godzilla, William Blake (the AMC version), or the old Hollywood set of Shangri-la – a lavish staged space of artificial waterfalls, technicolor rainbows, fathomless chasms. Yet often the truly visionary is a much quieter and sneakier affair; it occurs when a writer combines elements of story or observation in truly unexpected yet felt ways that somehow radically torque how we see our everyday world. I think, to cite one example of Shirley Jackson, whose odd combination of horror and coziness – leavened by her deep sense of what is meant by "family culture" – created a new vision of what horror could be, or how horror could be allied to a strange wonder and tenderness.

Similarly, with *The Glass City*, Jen Knox has written a series of fictions that speak with such acute – and, yes, tender – observation about who she is and where she is from; yet she adds to this the radical unpredictability of what used to seem like science fiction. These stories are squarely and deeply located in the landscape of the Midwest, the aging rust belt cities and towns, the proud, gritty, troubled, and rooted families that have grown up here. Yet in each one we feel the intrusion of the unpredictable, the catastrophic, the uncanny-ness that is our climate change world.

The precise proportions or ways in which Knox combines these elements feel very unique to her and manage to convince me – as a reader on multiple levels – about the texture, the interiority of her lives and characters in ways that get under my skin. I move from the page to think about how my own life is changing in real time thanks to climate change. I think about all the parts of this I have not been able to see or feel clearly enough. This experience happens not because of the fantastical in Knox's work, but because of how that fantastical – a seven-year drought in Ohio, a beyond humid Los Angeles where buildings simply cave in out of exhaustion – is so thrillingly bonded to details of the real – details of class, social habit, social hierarchy, and so on. In addition, Jen Knox's characters respond to what is coming in ways that never fail to take into account the precise circumstances – towns, cities, families – they have grown out of. The stories in *The Glass City* feel futuristic in some ways but are also so bonded to history, a sense of personal history, and it is this admixture that makes them peculiarly haunting as readers can see in a passage such as this one: "It was just the three of us and the still winter night, watching the river as we ate a simple dinner of chicken and corn on the cob. We discussed the movie we'd see next week and the test I had coming up in English, calculating our words, not mentioning how shallow the river water appeared. Even without discussion, it was the only conversation possible."

I reflect on the two sisters, Claire and Alette, in the beautiful story "Gathering the Ingredients," who following their mother's death try to honor her final instructions by travelling from the Midwest to open a bakery in a surreal war-torn Nice, France – a city collapsing into chaos because of migration and poverty due to climate change. Despite its many magical realist elements, the story draws us immediately into the sisters' world. Knox tells us of a game they used to play: "At one time, the sisters played a game that drove Jasmine crazy. They'd close their eyes, begin at the front door, and feel their way around the small home until they'd ventured to all rooms without a peek. The game would sometimes scare one or the other, a misstep would send electricity through their bellies, but they never cheated. Alette would reach out for her sister's hand." The game feels like the trust Knox creates in us as we accompany her through this book. At every step, we feel "yes, this is how it might be," or "this is how it is."

I read this book in 2017 when it was first published – it has since been revised with two new stories added. At that time, the radical climate disruption it described – the fear of pandemics and the mask-wearing and caution people must exercise just to live – felt more like science fiction than it does now, a handful of years later. I have the eerie sense of our everyday world moving rapidly to collide with hers, yet the visionary is about more than simply telling us what's coming, the way a good tarot reading is not about the future, but rather about providing a story of the present we can respond to in deep and perhaps unexpected ways, thereby, in some sense, liberating ourselves.

Put simply, reading *The Glass City* allows me to grasp with a more whole self what I see unfolding with my own eyes. For example, here where I write this in San Antonio, we are experiencing a heatwave, with seventeen days over 100 degrees in the last month, the hottest June ever on record. When I go into my garden, only the sunflowers are hanging on without water; each day another plant shrivels up and just gives over. Yet the stories in this book are not about despair, they are about the moments, like feeling the water in the hose in my yard go from bathtub hot to cool again as it trickles over my hands. The stories are about the sisters who trust the knowledge, the muscle memory they carry in their hands and fingertips: "They folded dough and eyed wax paper lined with their homemade truffles, prepared to instruction. They baked cookies and scones, mixed batters, and blasted French pop music as customers, one by one, began to line up in anticipation. The smells of fresh breads and sweet creams, of chocolate eclairs and almond macaroons, enveloped the sisters. They tied their aprons. Claire flipped the sign and unlocked the door."

There is not a story in this book I could not talk about in this way – that does not evoke its particular landscape with thrilling immediacy and intensity, so we understand a little more what it is to be here, to see and listen and feel what is "actually happening on this earth, at this time."

Sheila Black
Author of *All the Sleep in the World* and *Iron, Ardent*

THE GLASS CITY

The December sun threw white light against the SeaGate building, blanketing the Maumee River, as the neighborhood discussed the West Coast droughts. I was hoping the topic of conversation would change. I worked and waited, shivering against the crisp air that snuck through my bedroom window.

Dad's voice boomed, "We can't underestimate the damage it can do, even here. Never you mind the Dust Bowl, people forget the late '80s, and—"

"People are already hoarding. Bottled water sales are through the roof," Mom added. My parents were ganging up on someone. I glanced down to see my father lighting the grill.

Mr. Henry, a quiet, doughy man who lived two houses down and seemed a fixture in our backyard, stepped forward and mumbled for a long time. All I could make out were the words "Ohio" and "hope."

Dad caught my gaze and tipped his head, motioning for me to come down, before responding to Mr. Henry the same way he did when discussing the local economy and other perilous things, "That's all we can do, I guess. Work at what we love and wait for the good part."

I rolled my eyes, pushed my window down a sliver to ensure it was totally sealed, then put on a heavy coat and ventured downstairs. Thick slabs of meat, freshly chopped and pulsing, were ready for me. The sun skipped along the bellies of knives that were lined up on the sink near the door.

There were always three such knives on display when the neighborhood congregated in our backyard. One was for vegetables, a smallish spear-point knife with a delicate blade that required Mom's precision. Dad referred to the other two knives as brothers; the larger, a butcher knife, was my father's tool. He used it to prepare the steaks and chicken, but not until the grill was hot. The breaking knife, *the little brother*, would trim any remaining fat and was designed to cut down oversized pieces, prepare smaller portions for skewers – this was my job, to trim the fat.

A sheet of thin, cold air wrapped around me as I got to work. When I went to close the door, I saw Mom looking down at her phone. I knew what the text said by the way she shrugged and gave Dad her apologetic half-smile.

"Looks like I'll be eating leftovers," she said, up and through the doorway in no time, kissing me on the cheek. Mom was a surgeon then, well-respected in Toledo and unwilling to retire her scalpel, despite the threat of arthritis. I noticed the way she massaged her hands after long shifts, the increasing stock of sample-sized pain relievers living in our junk drawer.

Dad offered an appreciative smile, the smile he reserved for her alone, and turned to me. "Haley, are you getting down to work?"

"I'm on it," I said, treating the steaks with care and piercing them, along with small onions and green peppers. I painted portabellas with butter and garlic, and huddled near the fire with Dad and our neighbors, looking out at our quiet cityscape as discussions ranged from composting to cooking, then back to the droughts, not venturing inside until my toes turned to solid ice.

Later that evening, Dad told me he was impressed by the symmetry of my knife work. He had been a chef in an Italian restaurant for over a decade. It was a small and expensive restaurant that took a gut punch during the recession in 2008 but hung on longer than any other upscale restaurant nearby. It was downtown, close to the water, a favorite of most of the businesspeople who worked in proximity. After downsizing from a five-person kitchen to a single chef, my father, in 2013, La Trattoria closed for good.

Downtown was eerily quiet that Friday night. We were loud, arguing over what movie to see after dinner. My father paused when we approached his old restaurant. The storefront was boarded up and covered in sloppy graffiti. We were on our way to the SeaGate Restaurant. It was where my birthdays were often celebrated when I was younger, and we hadn't been there in years.

"Maybe it's time. Maybe I'll apply at the SeaGate. I'll consider this meal their interview," Dad said, fingering the short ponytail he'd grown since being out of work.

My father was hungry to cook, but despite his obvious skills, no high-end restaurants were hiring. He'd accepted a job at a chain restaurant for a time, only to find himself coated in disgust for the manner in which the food was prepared and served, half-hearted and half-done. He opted to take on construction gigs over low-end food service, but the SeaGate would fall somewhere in the middle, so it was a promising idea.

Another few blocks, and I was unnerved by the lack of people downtown. Toledo had been facing a recession for some time, but that night seemed extreme. When we arrived, we noticed there were no cars. A sign on the door said "Temporarily Closed Due to Drought."

"I didn't realize so many things were closing," Mom said. The hope I'd seen in my father's face flickered as she continued, "It hasn't affected the hospital much, but it's definitely hitting the news. Want to grill out?"

It was just the three of us and the still winter night, watching the river as we ate a simple dinner of chicken and corn on the cob. We discussed the movie we'd see next week and the test I had coming up in English, calculating our words, not mentioning how shallow the river water appeared. Even without discussion, it was the only conversation possible.

I was ten when my father got me a nylon knife set to teach me the basics. The knives were serrated, with blunt tips and soft handles. They were light and efficient when it came to slicing cake but disappointing when trying to cut anything that was yet to be cooked.

It didn't take long before I was using the real thing and imagining myself in the kitchen of a bustling restaurant. My father's German knife set with its wide, heavy blades, then the Japanese set with a lighter design that felt like air in my hands, became my playground.

Mom worried her hands as I learned to cut fish into thin sheets, sashimi style. After a few weeks' practice, I could carve carrots into flowers. I spent every minute outside of school working with my father in the kitchen. For a while, it seemed to energize him, so even after a long shift at La Trattoria, he'd be eager to teach me something new.

I cut myself for the first time two years after picking up that first knife set. I had been trying to chop cucumber as fast as Dad did, timing myself while he set up chairs outside for company. A diagonal slice of my index finger was removed in a nanosecond, and I stared down at the piece of skin for what must have been a long time before I realized how much I was bleeding.

Mom had been napping after a high-risk surgery on a woman whose tumor had been buried deep in her abdominal cavity. She'd gone over all the details when she came home. It had been a tricky operation, and Mom had worried that the woman was too small to be under anesthesia for so long. Although she had survived, and the tumor was successfully removed, Mom felt she had failed.

I hadn't wanted to wake her with my minor injury, so I did as I knew to do. I wrapped the finger tightly, putting pressure on it with a towel, as I searched the cupboard for the right container for my fingertip. I filled my father's coffee mug with ice and settled the tip inside, sure it would never be reattached, then went to find my father, who was greeting the first of our guests, a co-worker of his whom I'd never see again.

When my dad saw it, he woke Mom immediately. They drove me to the ER. Mom's team was eager to fix me, but it was clear that the fingertip was not salvageable. Perhaps I had looked at it too long, watching the yellow and red blob lying there like something foreign to me, until it became foreign to me.

By next spring, there was no denying the drought's impact. It had moved beyond conversation. I was soon to graduate high school, and our water fountains were all out of order. People complained that those upstream were siphoning the water, and Lake Erie would dry up within a few more months. There was an inordinate amount of red algae, which thrived in the shallow water and incessant heat.

There was talk of postponing my graduation, and the SeaGate still hadn't opened. Even fast-food restaurants were shutting their doors, and it seemed my father's lack of employment was becoming the norm.

I had been working all day on admissions applications to culinary schools, and one in Hawaii, a plush state unaffected by the drought, was my top choice. As I hit *save*, I thought about what it would be like to leave. I glanced outside at the dark-green river, which was low enough to reveal the tops of bicycles and large trash dumped in over the years, and I wondered what there'd be to come back to. I heard a knock, three beats and a pause. My parents were throwing a morale-boosting cookout, and I was done just in time.

I greeted Mr. Henry, who was wearing an unflattering white T-shirt, at least a size too big. Then a few other neighbors, all in tanks and T-shirts, uncharacteristic for this early in the spring, and I took my position in front of the knives. The grill was hot, and Dad nodded up at me as though we were old buds meeting in a bar.

"You've been working hard," he said.

I noticed the whiteness of my father's lips by the time Mom arrived home. There was a slight crack in his bottom lip, as though someone had made an incision. Mom unscrewed the top of a bottle of water and handed it to him without looking his way.

"No," he said. "I had mine." Just over the last week, the city had begun rationing water. We were all allowed two a day, and no one was allowed to buy in bulk. I'd caught my father pouring his water into my bottle more than a few times.

"They're restricting water in the trauma unit," Mom said sadly, when talk of the drought inevitably arrived. Noticing the way our faces fell, she sat down with asparagus and sweet potatoes, a delicate blade yielding to her touch, and changed the subject. "This might be the last of our produce for some time." She had already changed shirts but still wore her green scrubs, which were clean. Mr. Henry mumbled something about hope, and Dad smiled.

"Any good news?" he asked.

"No one had to be sliced open today," Mom said. She smiled, too, attempting to lift the mood. Her eyes grazed my father's lips. "Have you all heard about that family, a family just like us—a boy and his parents—who robbed a Sam's Club for all its water and hauled it off in a heavy-duty truck with stripped plates? I think that's why they're rationing here."

"Out of control," my father said, clapping his hands weakly as he began working the steaks. Mr. Henry set out paper plates and napkins. There was a spice mixture next to the sink. No salt.

"We'll do anything if we're scared enough," Jessica, who lived three houses down, said.

"Bet we're the only people in the entire city invited to a barbecue in the middle of the Dust Bowl," Mr. Henry chimed with an appreciative smile, then pointed to my parents.

My father gave a half-smile, then reached for the butcher, and he slowly began slicing the meat along the grain. Confused, I reached out to cover his hand with my own. The angled tip of my index finger could still feel, and as it pressed down against the roughness of his knuckles, I guided his hand to reposition the knife. "Across the muscle fibers. You taught me that," I said.

"The lighting in here is no good," Dad said.

"I know, Dad." The lighting was perfect.

He examined my finger. There was only a sliver of a nail that continued to grow over the nailbed. I liked to paint it; this day it was purple. "Hey, you know I'd rob a Sam's Club for you and your mother if it meant life or death. I'd do any absurd thing it took to keep you two hydrated."

"I know, Dad," I said, thinking about how quickly the term *hydrated* had changed meaning.

"You got all those applications in?"

I nodded.

Dad hadn't gone to culinary school. He'd been taught by a surly chef he did grunt work for while he was in high school. He worried that the economy would keep me from ever making a living wage, but I knew that Toledo, once an apex of glass-working techniques, was on the verge of a breakthrough. I had faith in our city.

I cut up a few strips for skewers as my father watched me, and said, "I'm getting good, eh?" I pushed the water bottle his way.

Dad smiled, and as he did, the crack in his lip broke, revealing the tender pink beneath it. He looked out at my mother, who was recounting her day like a soldier coming home from war. She massaged her hand as she spoke.

Her days, even slow days, were never mundane. She'd recount the patients and their families, so many personalities converging, and either stoic or panicked beyond belief when they entered her unit. She often spoke about her job as though selling it, and I saw a fleeting hint of disappointment when I told her I was going to culinary school.

She looked back, as though sensing my father's eyes. She looked at him the only way she could now, with gratitude and apology, then her gaze turned to me. I held up the plate of food and watched my father's triumph.

"Let's do what we do, kiddo. Let's feed the masses," he said.

The sun had no mercy as the heat wave bloomed the first few weeks of summer. We all hoarded water and squirreled away our resources. We figured out how much we needed to survive. The barbecues stopped, and we began to peek out windows before venturing anywhere, weighing the necessity of what we did. There was a constant lightheadedness.

My father never robbed a Sam's Club, but he was damn near mummified by the time the rain returned. Mom snuck him into a reserved room and hooked him up to an IV, but the damage had been done. The hospitals had become triage centers, ill-equipped for weeks that felt like years.

The way I remember the drought clearest is by reimagining the end. Children and adults alike rushed into the street during that first rainfall. They beamed up at the darkened sky and looked for open areas to outstretch their arms. No driver dared upset the harmony of the rain by venturing out onto the roads, and the Maumee rose the feet it had dropped. Those who had been driving pulled over and stood outside to absorb each drop.

The sun bounced off the wet ground and soaked the moisture quickly, but the water had already begun to heal, and forecasters expected more. As extremes blanketed the states, Toledo, once the booming Glass City, later a forgotten piece of the Midwest, became a haven. It received the first rain for hundreds of miles. The economy that had been carved open and cut to bits would be a foundation for renewal.

"The good part is coming," Dad said, as though he could see the future.

I saw it, too. As it continued to rain, I saw Dad tracing the spine of a fish with a paring knife in the kitchen of SeaGate. I saw Mom being called to the operating room for surgeries only her still-nimble and practiced hands could execute. I saw our knives lined up and waiting for the day I returned from culinary school, waiting for our next family cookout. The entire neighborhood would be invited. We'd stare out at the Maumee, our bustling reborn city, and we'd discuss something new.

THE LIVING MUSEUM

I sit cross-legged on the bus with a cloth grocery bag and notebook in my lap – trying to dismiss the urge to speak to the man next to me. He's over six feet tall, with no ring. Mouth agape and eyes fixed, he watches the reddening sky with everyone else. I watch him, longing to become a part of that sky.

The woman across the aisle points to the window when I look her way. I just nod and write. *My urges are part of a condition, not a part of me.* Meanwhile, the familiar squall of urgent desire drives out rational thinking as the impending storm bathes everyone in soft, flattering light. I drop my notebook and lean into the man, if slightly, to retrieve it.

My goal is to avoid triggers until I become stronger, but this requires meticulous planning – more planning than I thought, given the bus schedules and a rather inconvenient mistake I made some months back. The problem today is bigger than the man next to me, it's closer to home. My problem is numbers. Well, that and proximity.

I slept with Jack, my neighbor, who has sticky eyes and lifts his eyebrows often when he speaks to me, as though genuinely interested. Jack is a waiter with odd shifts. I knew he would be a problem when he moved in, but I successfully resisted his extended company. Well, until he invited me to an open-mic night on a particularly lonely Tuesday evening.

It's never the good poetry that gets me. Good poetry is a brief release, in fact, but good poetry is rare. Besides, there's something about bad poetry – I think it's the intensity in which the material is delivered, the naïve beauty translated, the human desire to be heard, seen, even if a voice is swathed in cliché and melancholy.

I've seduced many mediocre and unequivocally horrible poets in the last few years; so many, in fact, that my likeness appears in at least half a dozen chapbooks, which I keep in a small safe, along with my passport and divorce papers. I make it a point to buy and read as many literary journals as I can, searching for my depiction as though I were Waldo, lost in red and white – the conceptualized, hypersexual version.

I find it curious that, of those approached, no one has outright resisted my advances. Perhaps my suffering is just less passive. I am irresistible due to the slight curl to my upper lip, someone once said. Mom used to call me "Little Elvis."

I was a willing muse. It pained me to stop going to open-mic nights, but the museums and galleries really tugged at my soul. Long before I began treatment, I was a regular in the Gallery District. Often, a painting would propel me to grab a guard by his belt loop. "No touching," the best of them said. He still calls. I sometimes answer.

I haven't been in a while, but when I went, it was always something unexpected: an oil the size of a hardcover book – an abstract forest with richly colored angles – or a sculpture, a miniature armoire made of forks with an old boot resting atop. I talked about juxtaposition or color or dimension, and wondered how any person could go home to an empty bed night after night. I thought that shoe was at least a size eleven, and I imagined its owner.

Now I use graham crackers for Mr. Graham's intended purpose—to squash desire. I eat them plain, dunked in milk, and allowed to dissolve on my tongue in order to distract. I eat them one after another on particularly lonely nights. I eat them until they begin to taste like nothing. I have four boxes in my bag.

Entering a museum without willing the person next to me to slip his hand into the back pocket of my jeans is still a dream. One day, I'll be able to appreciate the art, the poetry. I'll be able to sit on this bus, next to this slender man – or one like him – and not even register the slow way he chews a piece of gum.

When one of the security guards I picked up at a gallery a few months ago showed up at Jack's apartment for a party, there were only eyes to tell stories, but it was this day – so close to home – that I decided to begin therapy three days a week. Most of my check goes to rent and therapy now, so I can't afford excursions. This works out well because the likelihood of two people I slept with showing up in a single location again is increasing.

Generally, I aim to arrive between four and five thirty to avoid Jack. I would make perfect time today, but the bus keeps stalling and people keep discussing the sky. When I finally reach my stop, a short man debuses before me.

I notice his shiny shoes moving quickly. His pants are worn at the bottoms – the contrast would catch any artist's eye; *this man is a walking painting*, I think, and I want to meet the painter. As we wait at the crosswalk, I see him examining my bag, so I offer him a graham.

He points toward the mass of red clouds moving along the panhandle. "Winds up to thirty miles per hour," he says, double-checking his phone to confirm. He smiles at me, an old gold filling winking dimly from the back of his mouth.

I still have the bag with the graham crackers pointed his way. He works the cardboard loose and takes one before walking off. As I watch him go, I finally notice the sky as everyone else does. People stand, staring.

I realize I don't have to wait at this crosswalk because there are no cars. Winds this strong and clouds this dense mean lost visibility, and drivers have pulled over. Red dust dances in the wind, and I have to blink fast to see anything until it settles.

"Be careful out there," the man yells from half a block away. He opens an industrial-sized umbrella before speed walking toward a pearl-colored Jetta, which confuses me. I want to run after him, to ask if I can borrow his big umbrella because it looks as though it could guard me from anything and might be able to double as a boat; the sky looks as though it is about to open up.

I wonder briefly what it would be like to curl up with the man in the back of the Jetta. I imagine a brown interior, soft. Instead, I hurry toward my apartment with the cloth grocery bag handle around my left wrist.

Summer-long droughts made the rains that began yesterday's headline news, but when the clouds turned red, while I was shopping for my grahams and humming to the brilliantly numbing sounds of The Smiths, panic began to rustle up around me. Now, those of us outside have our phones poised as though they are shields.

The online news is audible and all sermons – celebrity preachers praying for our souls. Then come instructions to get inside, blasting on all public speakers, creating an unsettling tone that will keep my ears ringing.

The rain is thickening, visible in the distance, falling in heavy clumps as though being squeezed out like dough. It is slowly violent, sealing people in their homes and cars. The best option is to run for a bridge, somewhere open but sheltered. Locking ourselves away in our homes appears a death sentence.

People are abuzz, gossipy flies. Someone says it is a mixture of volcanic ash and sludge. The thickness may be due to the humidity and wind.

"They say there's an extreme heat wave following this craziness." Jack's voice is not deep, not rough. Still, it echoes. He is wearing a large coat with a checkered lining that peeks out from the collar. Thick clothes make sense. He posts pictures to social media and asks me to pose for a selfie with him, selling it like this: "It might be your last one." I wave him off, say I'll take a quick shot of him instead. "Put on the filter," he says.

"Are you kidding? Selfies in Pompeii?"

"This lighting is great," he says.

It looks as though he is standing in front of a green screen, a garishly fake background behind him – as though he was supposed to be on Mars or in the middle of, well, the apocalypse. He stands smiling, waving at me as though it's been years, and I feel a familiar nudge to grab him and tell him this is it – our final days – so why not?

"Take a few," he says; his narcissism breaks the spell, if only momentarily. Perhaps I wouldn't have to avoid Jack if I got to know him well enough.

"You realize this might be pointless? These clouds will erase us all," a woman says through gritted teeth. She holds her hand out and a stray dollop of clay lands in her palm. As it expands, she tries to peel it off but cannot.

I drop my grahams. News blares over loudspeakers, and a message flashes across all mobile screens. I hear and see nothing until someone yells, "The rain is turning people into fucking statues!"

Becoming fucking statues could be nirvana.

Jack grabs my hand, pulls hard. It feels like a slow, cool shower. It feels like a thick bath. It is seductive, a coating of cool paint. My feet begin to stick, and I lift one to find myself leaning forward, but I fight to reposition. I tense every muscle, focus, but soon I am immobilized to the ankles, then calves. Jack is stuck on his knees.

It happens quickly, with a wave of heat. I feel my skin pulling toward the clay, beginning to dry, and I struggle to control what I can – to reach for Jack's hand. In mere hours, we are solid, and begin to crack in the Texas sun.

Some say we still look alive, that our shells just needed to be chipped away to reveal the life within, but these people are regarded eccentrics by others. They all speculate in some way, however, because when we engage them, they become transfixed. They are captured in a moment, relieved of all urges, if briefly.

No one will take photos at The Living Museum, but people will arrive in droves to meet us. They will surmise different scenarios, cite erroneous sources, touch when guards are not looking, guess, and claim to know our relationships. Meanwhile, when they arrive, we will watch them and their world as though they are the ones on display. We will continue to watch, just as they always dreamed someone would.

EMOTIONAL INTELLIGENCE

Imagining her feet rooting down into the linoleum, Emerson stood upright, barely, in line at the grocery pharmacy. Since she'd forgotten her cane, her failsafe, she had to focus. The vertigo, which had plagued her since she was sixteen, intensified as an announcement requested a cleanup in the bakery.

Maybe after filling this prescription, as her mother had, she would have an ordinary life, the kind that allows one to luxuriate in personal ailments alone. She looked forward to simple neurosis, a few obsessive habits, willful laziness, or narcissistic tendencies that would keep her company and offer consistency. Whatever form, they'd be hers alone. Until then, the problem was everyone else.

Within a ten-foot radius, she was exposed to the anger of an elderly woman in front of her, the deep depression of a balding pharmacist, the repressed rage of whoever was making announcements, and the wild energy of impatient twin redheads who stood beside a large and happy man who was waiting for a robust blood pressure medication.

Emerson reached forward, settling her hand on a sloped shoulder. The woman was around seventy, and her posture resembled Emerson's cane so acutely that she could have been the personification of its twisted cherry wood and engraved knob. That is, until Emerson felt the shoulder go rigid and hot.

She apologized but couldn't move her hand. The woman's face softened as she examined Emerson through hooded eyes. "I don't blame you for dozing off. We'll be here all goddamn day," she said.

A dense orange light around the woman told Emerson a patchwork story: a bus stop with a dirty bench, where the woman's beige trench coat picked up a large smudge. Each step of a painfully slow walk to the Customer Service desk where four lottery tickets and trail mix were purchased every Saturday before another painful walk here, to the pharmacy line. Other days, other errands. There were doctors' offices, post offices, bus stops, long rides, and a well-worn chair on a concrete-slab of a front porch in a low-rent retirement community.

Taking a deep breath, Emerson gestured toward a man leaving the line. "I think it'll pick up now," she said, delicately removing her hand.

"Yeah right." The woman didn't introduce herself, but Emerson saw her name, Beatrice, on her prescription. Beatrice's energy was fierce and fleeting, and Emerson breathed it in to steady herself and quiet the other messages that were bombarding her.

Emerson's doctor had prescribed an anti-anxiety medication, one of myriad suggested medications, after her last incident, a supposed panic attack that landed her in the hospital after a trip to Starbucks. Though she was hesitant to fill the prescription, the heart palpitations and dizziness were too much. Something had to change.

When Emerson was eight, it felt like a gift. To read others' energy more acutely told her who to play with and who to avoid. It was fun to share in the sheer delight of her dog before he was fed, or the younger children whose awe preceded them – those whose presence was so soft that it even felt nourishing when they were emotional.

When Emerson's mother and grandmother sat around the kitchen table wearing robes with towels wrapped tightly around their heads and green clay masks on their faces, Emerson would ride high on the airiness of their good humor for hours. She used to play with her grandmother's cane, dancing around it, not realizing how necessary it was.

Then the day came that her father walked into the living room and dropped his bag. She could see his life fading, a deep stillness that surrounded him. Her sister didn't see it; her friend, Jenny, told her she was an oddball when she tried to explain that something was wrong with her father. He was his jovial self, after all, making jokes and laughing loudly. But Emerson could see that he was ailing like the old pine in their backyard.

As she got older, the sensations became more acute. The colors were brighter and emotions louder. In some ways it worked out. She could read people. Reaching her early twenties, Emerson got every job she applied for. She sailed through marketing classes at an online college and quickly started making six figures at a consulting firm where she wanted to connect with coworkers, but it was too much.

The office was filled with a weighty collective apathy intermixed with guilt and competitiveness. So, she petitioned to offer her services online and would read sample audiences' responses over video with such insight that she had to lie here and there to stay on promotion track.

She tried online dating a few times. She requested a man named Jay meet her in a small café, but realized the high-strung barista was too distracting. Although Jay seemed nice enough, she couldn't keep eye contact or pay attention to what he was saying and felt his self-consciousness turn to defensiveness. The next few dates, which took place at parks or libraries, were either needy or overconfident, ending with unraveling stories of repression or delusion. She saved money, had her food and clothes delivered, and only went to this grocery if it was before sunrise. That is, until today. The pharmacy opened at 7 a.m.

"We're all on a journey. Stay the course," Emerson's grandmother once told her before unlatching a necklace she wore every day; it was a small silver bird floating on a thin chain. She laced the cool silver around Emerson's neck and kissed her forehead. "When we figure everything out, we begin to harmonize, then we go home."

"We are home," Emerson argued, tracing her thumb over the bird and reaching out to touch her grandmother's long gray curls. It was winter, and Emerson wore a Sleeping Beauty nightgown that felt like a cloud.

"No. We're far from home, kiddo."

Her grandmother's embrace was a profusion of color and grace.

A honey-baked ham special was announced, and customers funneled toward the deli. Emerson took a few steps forward and felt the whirlwind again. A thin man stood behind her, his hand tapping his thigh. She turned to see that one of his headphones was hanging by his side, and he grinned, looking down at her feet. Nick. His name was all she got and that came from the embroidery on his shirt pocket.

"Come on, hon," Beatrice said, taking a few steps forward and reaching for her hand. "Are you steady now?"

Emerson smiled and followed along, getting a small surge of compassion, but she was bothered by the lack of energy around Nick. There was nothing, no light or lack thereof.

Beatrice leaned against the counter, sliding her credit card over to a pharmacist who offered a half smile and answered a lot of questions. Most of the answers began with "Like I told you last time," but Beatrice was impenetrable. Her straight gray hair was thin and tucked neatly behind her ears. Her bus wouldn't arrive for another ten minutes, so she had words to burn. The pharmacist stared blankly.

Nick began to cough through closed lips, choking back his illness. "Pardon me," he said, and the hacking continued. His face reddened slightly.

Emerson narrowed her eyes, searching, and then she saw it. "Want to go ahead?" she asked, stepping aside.

The young man coughed through his answer, waved off her proposition, and placed a hand on her back, gently. She didn't feel anything from this man. She noticed his tall posture and loose arms, the way he moved easily even though he was obviously ill.

"Stay the course." Emerson heard her grandmother's voice. Her grandmother, who hadn't died but rather sauntered toward death. Her grandmother, who never seemed tortured by her gifts but somehow enchanted by them.

Emerson tried to picture this man's day job at a factory and nights studying at community college, his desire to enter a corporate world that he'd hate if he ever encountered it, and his large and loving family who would be by his side over this next year, but this was all made up, a story in her mind. There was no clue, no energy to absorb. He was contained.

Beatrice waved goodbye, her step just a beat lighter. Emerson's prescription was ten dollars, and it came with warnings of drowsiness and dizziness, which she laughed at. She shook the bottle as she walked out of the pharmacy. Ice cream was BOGO half off, a new voice announced, as Emerson approached the exit. She glanced back, locking eyes with Nick, who was standing at the pharmacy counter, neck craned to watch her go. No expression. He was trying to figure her out, too.

Emerson felt a new wave of emotions as she joined those walking to and from their cars, gathering carts, and occupying the gas station nearby. She steadied herself on a shopping cart before making her way to her car. The locks released, and she settled into the leather seat. Leaning back, she breathed in the solitude and felt her body reset as though being restarted.

The pills were small and menacing. She turned one over, rolling it between her index finger and thumb. Just as she was about to place it in her mouth, a knock arrived at the door, and the young man, Nick, waved.

She rolled down the window and waited.

"You dropped this," he said as his thin fingers separated, allowing the silver chain to fall into her hand. The pains and worries, avoidance and impatience she'd ingested over the last twenty minutes funneled out of her body as she clasped the necklace and felt her throat release.

"Grandma sent you."

Nick smiled, but she couldn't see his intention, couldn't feel his illness. It was as though he didn't truly exist. She watched him walk evenly toward his car, dropped the pill in the bottle, and lifted her hand to her heart as he waved. It beat powerfully, rhythmically, as the world raged on.

GATHER THE INGREDIENTS

At one time, they believed in fairy tales. They believed in the burnt sugar-scented cobblestone dreamland that came to life in their mother's stories. They stayed up nights discussing life as though it were a soft, sweet thing to sample, like the truffles that cooled on wax paper in their kitchen. The perfect, plump chocolates were just waiting to be plucked by tiny fingers. Claire snuck two as Alette drew Pâtisserie Jasmine, a pastel cottage perched on a round green hill.

At forty and thirty-nine, the sisters waited in long Customs lines that ended with exhaustion and petulance. They argued over directions. Claire examined the map on her phone as Alette hailed a cab.

The driver eyed their bags, stopped twenty feet ahead of them, and popped the trunk as he idled. His car contained a layered aroma, the tarragon and sage remnants of a sophisticated lunch settling atop the sourness of upholstery that had absorbed too many spills. The cab weaved through heavy traffic beneath a swollen pre-storm sky. The sisters shared a tattered seat in silence.

Both Claire and Alette had been by their mother's side when she passed. By the time Alette had arrived, however, Jasmine was already in a medicinal haze, teetering on the edge of life. Claire, who had been there every day since the diagnosis, every possible hour in fact, had settled in denial. A doctor had to ask that she remove her hand from her mother's limp wrist. Now, some weeks later, there was no room to deny, and the pain was nestling inside them both. Sitting rigidly as the cab traversed increasingly bumpy and circuitous roads, they neared their hotel,

Jasmine, unlike her daughters, had been prepared. She'd known long before any diagnosis or ill feeling. She told Claire that she had dreamed the number thirteen. It was a marzipan thirteen, and she'd devoured it – despite her aversion, despite a sickness that ultimately caused her to fall over in the dream.

"I fell to wakefulness and knowing," she'd said. Shortly after the dream, Jasmine began to write to her daughters – leaving them detailed instructions and narratives in the form of recipes. She had even directed them here with a box of loose notes that were to be compiled and shared.

Claire kept her mother snug in a silver urn swathed in a canvas bag that she now hugged to her chest like a child. She'd defended her mother's presence to TSA, then Customs. Jasmine had insisted on coming along in whatever form she could. She'd written to them, asking that her ashes be spread on the flower beds outside her old pastry shop.

A distant cousin, Marc, had struggled to keep the shop afloat. He kept it limping along for a few years, but the neighborhood was changing, he'd explained, and he had to move for the safety of his family since the terror attack in 2016. He'd tried to manage from a distance, only to fail miserably. When the sisters told him of Jasmine's request, he said it was impossible. "No natural things live in that neighborhood anymore. Not since the soldiers moved in. I've been trying to get your mother to sell for years."

If the sisters agreed on anything, it was that Jasmine *would* know if they didn't carry out her wish. They were hesitant but determined, unable to factor in the social climate. There was a feeling of something thickening the air, making it hard to breathe. It was a pervasive feeling that neither sister could deny, but it wouldn't stop them.

The silence was too much for Alette. She had a habit of filling space. She leaned forward and said to the driver, "How's business here?" When he didn't answer, she continued. "Cabs are almost obsolete in New York, you know. They've been overtaken by Uber."

The driver mumbled something, then began waving his hands at someone cutting him off. "Uber," he said with disgust before turning up his music, something jazzy and soft.

"Yep. Do you have that here?"

When there was no response, Alette looked to her sister. "I guess that means *yes*." Her gaze wasn't returned. She tilted her head on the glass, just before the driver slammed the brakes for the last time that evening. Her head jerked back.

"Asshat!" Claire said, reaching out to her sister. "Are you all right?"

"You know what I think of you?" the cab driver growled.

"I'm fine. Ignore him," Alette said. She handed him the fare as Claire got out of the cab and slammed the door.

The hotel was something from a movie, perhaps dirtier and droopier, but equally grand. It was a building Jasmine had described to them many times, a place where business executives and movie stars used to stay when they visited the French Riviera. It was a block from the theater, two blocks from Jasmine's old shop.

A concierge met the sisters at the trunk. He handled their bags with nimble movements and smiled with what seemed pure delight. His energy offset the anger of the driver, and it seemed to settle Claire some. The balconies of the hotel were painted white, and only a young couple stood outside, staring out at the Mediterranean with melancholy slouches and fixed gazes. This couple might've been the only other guests, as there was no one without a nametag in the lobby, no rustling sounds or tapping of feet. Only theirs.

Claire's tennis shoes squeaked in the foyer. She caught a few glances from hotel staff. Ever since the split from the husband, she had felt out of alignment. She caught eyes on the thin, untanned line on her finger, even as it seemed almost faded to nothing now. People no longer wanted to look her in the eye because there was something broken there, and when they did catch her gaze, pity wafted her way like a stench. When she reached the counter, she set her mother down gently and offered a forced smile to the woman who checked them in.

Alette's heels tip-tapped as she strode a few paces behind her sister. Jasmine, in her reverie, had convinced Alette that she was on the precipice of a big break, and ever since this drug-induced and late-arriving acceptance, she walked with her head even higher – almost to the point of awkwardness. Jasmine's belief was something special. She had lived in her heels and lifted the world with her smile, had run two businesses for many years, and had raised two daughters on her own.

Alette looked a lot like her, soft features and tiny shoulders. Claire was boxier, the puzzle piece that fits too many ways and is judged by utility alone, but Claire had inherited the work ethic. Holding her mother with both hands now, as though Jasmine were an offering, Claire and two of the hotel staff led the way to the room, with Alette lingering behind to appreciate the décor, then check her phone.

"Dear Artist: We thank you for your audition, but..." Alette deleted email after email, then moved on to the fourteen texts waiting for her. One was from her landlord, a final notice. George Watson, an exceedingly wealthy but impatient man, had been threatening to kick her out the last few months. She'd managed to get by a while by flirting, but he was no longer responsive to her efforts.

She tried for sympathy in a short instant message, then texted hearts to her girlfriend, as Claire tried to hand her the second key. After hitting *send*, Alette realized her jet lag must've gotten the better of her. All of the texts had gone to George, and, not knowing what else to do, she shut off her phone, hoping that somehow they wouldn't go through.

Claire cleared her throat in an attempt to get her sister's attention. When Alette didn't acknowledge her, Claire reached back and gave Alette's tiny shoulder a good squeeze. She said, "Come on, sis. We have work to do."

"*Oui*," Alette said, looking up. "*Pour maman.*"

Jasmine's estate comprised a bakery in Athens, Ohio, and a dilapidated building in Nice; at one time, both of Jasmine's shops would have sold for enough to cover the sizable mortgage she'd taken out on her home a year before the girls' father died, leaving only debt. Now, with business steady but stalled in Athens and halted completely in Nice, there was a lengthy climb, and some tough decisions to make.

The sisters had been left everything equally. Originally, Jasmine had planned to bring her girls to Nice herself, but after the dream, she transferred all her money to a small bond. They'd agreed to read them all once they made it to the hotel, before they saw the shop, and despite their previous exhaustion, neither sister felt tired in the least.

"You want to?" Claire asked.

"One or two. I might break down. Claire, I might break down, and if I do, be nice."

"Of course," Claire said, with mild irritation lacing her voice.

Girls, I am smiling on you if you are in France. If you are not, please get there. I'll wait. So, listen, the shop is a shell of its old self, and I don't blame you if you sell it, but before you do, try and fix it up. Clean it up, and after you've done so, I'd like you to make something. Macaroons. Sugarcoat the neighborhood, allow people to breathe it in. Just a batch. Try because I asked for so little when I was alive. Try because I will smell your efforts, too. Leave me with the flowers, with the shop where I gained independence. I'll greet people at the door, make them forget about the horrors of the world. Follow my recipe exactly! To a T.

She'd said as much to the girls in her final days. Jasmine wielded guilt like a sword, slicing away her daughters' hesitancy to follow her instructions. She had lived in Nice from age thirteen to sometime in her mid-twenties, after growing up in Cleveland, where her parents catered to the "fancies" by selling whatever they could at their pop-up shop. She learned business those years, but she never spoke highly of her time in Cleveland. Or of her parents, who were good at business but had no concept of planting roots, and eventually left their daughter with her grandparents. Her years in France, however, were delicate tales that melted on the tongue.

"Mom, loosen up, you should remember you're from *Nice*," the girls used to joke when she was upset, when things seemed impossible for a single mother of two. And she would chase them around their small living room – insisting that she'd show them how *neeece* she was. They'd giggle and clutch their stomachs, each trying to out-laugh the other, then they'd help with the next batch of pastries by watching, nodding, and handing their mother ingredients on cue. Claire was always a little faster to respond, a little more accurate with the measurements; Alette was always more enthusiastic.

Before she was hospitalized, Jasmine had told the girls she still had faith in the revitalization of her shop, the neighborhood she loved, but her faith was waning. "Probably, the tension will be there awhile. The world is headed this way. But things change. Princesses, small nudges do big things."

She had explained that the shop she owned was the size of a booth at the flea market, but that it was still legally hers. No one had tried to buy it. Her cousin, Marc, had taken over the shop after Jasmine married a man from Ohio who would be too perfect to not love, who would seduce her into returning to the States, who would die in a head-on collision on his way home from work shortly after Alette was born.

Marc had tried to manage the business for a while but had no patience for baking and no administration skills whatsoever. He hired teenagers and treated them poorly. They stole, so he fired them and hired more. Then he moved an hour away. He called one day to admit he couldn't keep it up. He suggested Jasmine sell. He suggested again.

The sisters stood on the balcony, both in blue jeans. The neighborhood did need the smell of macaroons. It smelled of rot and something sour. Guns lining their hips, three soldiers were patrolling the area on foot. Claire was studying the men when she heard the ding of her instant messenger. It was Alex. "You can't not answer," he wrote.

"I'm settling Mom's estate," she texted. She almost added, "Asshole," but deleted the second text, for legal reasons alone. Claire had caught her husband with a blonde woman whose round, pink ass bounced in full view on Claire's bed. When she'd found them, she said, "Divorce," then walked for miles. Simple, clean. Then again, it was anything but.

"I didn't know," he wrote. A few seconds later: "If I had known…"

The sisters read another of their mother's short letter-recipes.

Stop messing with my masterpieces now that I'm gone, Alette. No sugar-free, no fat-free. I'm not there to fix your mistakes. Macaroons: 2/3 cup almond meal, 1 1/2 cups powdered sugar, 3 large egg whites (keep them room temperature), 5 tablespoons granulated sugar, and 1 teaspoon vanilla. You need heat, but not too much. 280 degrees. Baking sheets, parchment paper—you know this much, Girls. Get the almond meal and powdered sugar in a food processor, mix till fine. Sift it. Sift it again. Medium-high speeds will beat those egg whites (Claire, if you still claim to be allergic, get over it). When the eggs froth, add granulated sugar 1 tablespoon at a time (Alette, you need to be patient, honey, don't just throw it all in there, got it?). Continue to beat the egg white mixture until it grows nipples when you lift the beaters. Gently stir in the vanilla extract. Don't overbeat, Alette!

"She thought I was developmentally challenged. Till the end, that is. She saw something change, she said."

Claire laughed. "You had a period there."

"Whatever. Everyone does. I wasn't asking for your opinion," Alette said. She paced. "I have to post about this. I feel so overwhelmed."

"Did you really just say that?" Claire asked, attempting to knock the thing from Alette's hands as she was telling her online friends that she'd arrived and was feeling down.

"This is how people do. This is how people process now, Claire. Transparency. You act like an old lady."

Alette was stretching on the balcony in the morning, finding humor in the catcalls directed at her. She could just as easily have stretched inside. Claire was telling her as much when the hotel staff rang the room to ensure they were awake.

Claire answered, asked that two cappuccinos be brought to the room. She noticed that her cell was flashing and checked to find a message from Alex: "Sorry again," that had come in last night, late.

Hoping the neighborhood was softer in the light, she glanced out the window. There were two men yelling up at her sister.

"Alette, doesn't that bother you?"

"Hey, you have the round ass. I like you," one of the men said to Claire when she stepped outside.

"Listen," she yelled down. "You two ass clowns can go harass someone else." She looked over at Alette, who had her feet positioned comfortably behind her head. "You eat that stuff up, don't you? You know it isn't a positive type of attention, right? You do realize they're just assholes who won't give you a second look when you turn forty, right?"

"I'm almost forty, you're forty," Alette said, "and they still seem dazzled by us."

"Whatever. Marc said he'd meet us at eight, but that probably means nine or ten, right?" The two men were yelling something that the sisters didn't understand, and two officers appeared out of nowhere to hurry them off.

"A lot of protection. They must know something we don't," Alette said, motioning to the policemen. She waved at them from her twisted position; they waved back, curious expressions on their faces.

Marc wasn't known for punctuality – another reason he'd given up the business. He called at noon. "I'm on my way. Meet me out front? I wear the red hat now, everywhere, in honor of your mother," he said. "I'll meet you at her place. I am not allowed in your hotel."

The sisters walked past the old shop, which was nestled between a salon and what looked like a condo. Claire dusted off the sign out front. There was a single window, a small sill.

"There could be some potential," Alette suggested.

"Riiiiight. Let's try the door."

The knob jiggled when turned, threatening to fall off. Marc had the key, and the locks hadn't changed in over a decade. But it seemed locks were useless. The door opened with a solid push.

Inside were dust, cobwebs, rust, remnants of squatters, and an upturned milk carton with something sticky coating it. Beneath this layer, there was, in fact, potential. There was a strong counter with a small oven behind it that had no dials and a broken door handle. There was the smell of decay and mold and something foul—perhaps something dead, but there was also a fridge. There was a small square of wood behind the counter that had their mother's initials carved into it. This made the sisters smile.

"I don't think we'll be making macaroons here, Mom," Claire said.

"She must have been on top of the world when she bought this place. It must have been beautiful then," Alette said. "We need to clean up. Can you imagine buying this at a time when women didn't own shit?"

Punch the center of the batter, then scrape more batter from the sides to the center, and punch it down again. Don't be afraid to really force it down. You will need to repeat this to strengthen it. If the batter is too runny, the macaroons will be oily, and the angels will throw spears at you girls. You have to continue on. Don't get ahead of yourselves. Don't try to rush it.

Claire got another text from Alex as they waited to see a red hat. "Let's put everything on hold. I need to talk to you."

Jasmine had liked Alex. She'd defended his infidelity – saying that men were weak and it was up to the women to forgive sometimes. "So long as there are no illegitimate babies, take him back! Easy," she'd said. "Then you have a free pass if you ever get tempted." Claire had been outraged at the suggestion that infidelity was a trading card. She remembered stomping out of the hospital room like a child, only to return with iced green tea and peanut butter sandwiches an hour later, calmed but no less offended.

"She liked you, too," she typed, then powered her phone off.

"I think this place has potential. Look, the oven works," Alette said. "There's electricity. Why is there electricity?"

"Marc must be paying for it. Try the lights."

"Claire, I need to do something different. Maybe we should fix it up and move here. Or I could move here."

"What do you know about running a business?"

"We know the business. It's in our blood. We can improve it. Macaroons, pies, cakes. I've been experimenting with a reduced-sugar version of a few things. She added too much sugar," Alette said. "Maybe some gluten-free."

"Mom's listening, Alette. Can you imagine?"

"I take it all back," Alette said, looking toward the ceiling.

"She missed you so much. It stressed her out that you weren't around."

"Whoa! Where'd that come from?"

Work together, Girls. Claire, get a pastry bag, pour it in. On your baking sheets (your prepped baking sheets), go at it. Bring those babies to life! Holding the baking sheet in both hands, smack it down on the counter a few times, so they don't get saggy. Go have a cigarette or do something. Ten or fifteen minutes, probably fifteen. Let them dry out. Have another cigarette or whatever while they bake, then let them cool, and you're ready for the ganache.

When they would work summers in their mother's Athens kitchen, measuring and blending ingredients was torture; Alette, with her thick eyeliner and all-black clothes, blue-black hair, and bruised attitude, would often sneak away early to smoke weed in a park near Ohio University. Claire, the overworked victim who had to take on yet another of her mother's catering gigs or finish another of Alette's abandoned shifts, did so at the cost of band practice. Playing catering captain during a fancy dinner full of stuffy people instead of charging the stream of sound, she endured. As a girl, Claire had clocked a lot of hours feeling sorry for herself.

The sisters had seemed anything but grateful at first. Even as adults, they were hesitant to help their mother with the business, until Claire caught Alex with the hefty blonde and knew she had to do something, to reevaluate her life. She finally began to help, and ended up running the shop long before she was ready. It was when she took over that she became a hypocrite, resentful of Alette, who was off chasing odd dreams and warped rainbows instead of helping their mother, even though she too had been chasing other things until said things turned on her.

"Look!" Alette said, reaching for a long rectangular flowerpot that was designed for the front. "It'll fit. We have to find flowers."

Marc arrived in a red hat, with gifts and flourish, a loud "Haylooo" and outspread arms. He had two tiny gift bags that carried scarves, were identical in pattern, and varied only in color, and he handed Alette the one with more purple tones and Claire the one with more greens. "For your eyes."

They each offered a hug and kiss. His unshaven cheek scraped their lips gently. "You look so distinguished and handsome," Alette said.

"Distinguished means old, no? Indeed!" he said, straightening his coat with the palm of his hand and smiling wryly. "I tried, ladies. I tried so hard with this place. It conspired against me. I kept paying the bills because I thought I'd have the time to clean it up." He grabbed a towel that was kept in a cabinet and began working at the countertops. "How'd you get in?"

"Wasn't hard. We need new locks," Claire said.

"I'll take care of it." He dusted off two wooden chairs and took a seat. "You two came here, even with all the travel warnings. I can't believe you really came." He traced the wood where Jasmine's initials were carved.

"Of course. I'm so happy to see you, Marc. How's Jessy?" Claire asked.

"Beautiful. I'm a lucky man. You two must come over while you're here. She bought fish. We would've put you up. Our new place is small and pretty far away. You can take the train."

"I like the hotel," Alette said.

"You might want to find one a few miles away."

"Is it that bad? We noticed the soldiers, the police."

"I don't know. Things seem okay, then they're not. There are no threats of bombs, then there are. Then they're dismissed. We are a paranoid people."

"We need to sell this place," Claire said, eyeing her sister.

Marc nodded along. "I don't want this place, but I want it to live. Since you're here for days and the tourist attractions take hours, we could clean. You can see the potential. Maybe you are better to sell it than I was?"

The three cleaned the counters while listening to Adele from Marc's iPhone and singing along sloppily, laughing the way they used to when they were kids. Had Jasmine been here, she'd have told them all to start acting like adults, only to begin dancing and singing along in her too-high heels. She wore heels almost every day of her adult life, even as her posture became a question mark.

After the oven was scrubbed and scoured, they decided to do as Jasmine had asked. "Marc, where is this store?" Claire asked, showing him their mother's letter. He began reading, chuckling.

"I miss her irreverence," he said. He took some time with the letters, turning off the music as his expression fell. The sisters traded a look and allowed him some time; they knew this look. Marc had been in denial, too, until now.

As they began putting the cleaning supplies away, Claire heard the faint ring of her phone. The Zoom call was from Alex. She stepped outside to answer.

"I'm so sorry," Alex said.

"I don't have time," she said.

Claire stood outside, half-listening, imagining violets the texture of felt out front. Her mother had loved those flowers, absorbing the slight moisture of the petals with her thumb, then dragging her thumb along her daughters' cheeks as though casting a spell.

"Your mother still spoke to me," he said, as though hearing her thoughts. "She was working on a plan to get us back together. I thought I'd try to carry it out on my own when she passed, but you can be a tough cookie."

"A tough cookie? You can be a lying asshole."

"I know, Claire. I know. But not anymore. Can we not stop this?"

"No, Alex. We cannot stop it." Alex and Claire had met at the grocery. Nothing special, no fun, romantic story, simply two people looking at pears; Claire for a warm dessert her mother wanted to try with heavy whipping cream and cinnamon, and Alex because he loved pears – or so he'd said. Another lie.

"Who are you talking to?" Alette asked.

When Claire mouthed *Alex*, Alette smiled. "What a mess that guy is. Make him pay, sis. Tell him he has to pay you for his infidelities. If Sandy ever cheated on me, I'd replace her shampoo with glue. I'd rig her office chair so that it sounded like she was farting every time she got up."

"I miss your sister," Alex said with a sigh. "Please don't do those things. Unless you are willing to forgive. Then you can do those things. Well, the glue would be bad because I'd look horrible bald. It's unfortunate because I think my hair is thinning. Claire, what will I do without you?"

She laughed a little, despite herself. He always rambled on. Nonsense that made her smile. She didn't answer. Looking up, distracted by her confused emotions, she saw three men with handguns running down the street, followed by a cluster of soldiers with rifles, then armored vehicles. It was a war parade, and one of the men yelled at Claire to stay indoors when he saw her. "Get inside now!"

When she went back inside, she was gasping for breath as though she'd just run. "Where's Marc? There are men outside," she began. There was a loud noise, like a hammer against the sky. Alette said Marc had gone to the store to get some ingredients.

Wispy light gray smoke entered the shop, but the sisters hardly noticed. It was coming from elsewhere, mostly kept out by the building. Another loud sound, a shot, rattled their hearts.

It soon became clear that the smoke was gaining momentum. A thick black mass covered the ceiling, and it began descending – far more violent than whatever had awakened it. Claire reached around for her sister, as she used to when they were children. "Come on," she said, inhaling tiny knives.

There was a time when the sisters felt almost like a single entity, each of them content in matching over-worn, over-sized sweaters on those winter days when the Midwestern air whistled and stung. Claire's was purple with pink hearts, and Alette's was the inverse. Back then, people often asked Jasmine if they were twins, and the girls would nod yes, giggling conspiratorially as their mother explained that, although they were close in age, they were far from twins. They used to reach for the other's hand any time life became too big.

Alette coughed, reached out. The sisters' fingers found each other, and when they gripped hands, Claire led Alette to the back door. The smoke was outside as well, but uncontained. People were running toward the water as though they were on fire. Buildings for half a block down smoked like giant chimneys. Soldiers were running in bird-like formations. Fire trucks drove in, and firemen got to work.

They ran. Alette's shoes did not slow her down. Marc's red hat was seen first near the grocer's, and when he turned around, the sisters ran faster still. He was looking dazed but standing in a clearing where the smoke began to lose its grip. They ran through the gradations as he ran toward them. Passing glazed doormen and a few security guards who were looking down the street as though trying to decide if they could help, they made their way toward the hotel. The air was clear here.

"A fire. Someone shot off a gun," the concierge from the other night said. He looked as though he was wearing a drama mask, his face tugged down from lack of sleep. Claire reached around to find her phone, but it was gone. Alette had hers in her back pocket, and the girls hunched over it to get the news. The power was flickering in the hotel. The staff was debating whether to lock the doors. One of them said that there were Americans, a couple, so it might be best to lock up and watch out for them.

The couple Alette had watched as they watched the sea, so awestruck and knowing, might have been killed. Forty-eight killed, said the American news app. Possible terrorism, not confirmed. *How could they know?* There was live footage of the smoke, and there were close-ups of a man in all black entering the theater. "Why did they get this footage? How did they get this footage and not intervene?"

Jasmine would not be spread on flowers, because nothing alive grew on that street anymore, but she would know they tried. The sisters announced their status by way of phone call and email to the American Embassy. Claire texted Alex from Alette's phone to let him know she was alive, and he texted back right away. "Love you, C. Love you more than ever." Alette fumbled to text a few of her friends and her girlfriend, but before she could get a response, her phone powered off.

"Shit! My charger was in my purse."

The sisters heard a loudspeaker announcement that warned everyone not to go out onto the balconies. Every building within a two-

59

mile radius was locked down. They suspected a suicide bomber on the run. Hotels were a prime target, as were anywhere large groups of people gathered. Claire began to cry. "Mom was in her shop. I left the bag there."

Crying softly, Alette sat next to her sister and eased her ear on her sister's shoulder. "I'm not afraid," she said. "I know we'll need to leave, but I'm not giving up."

"Me either."

When they returned to the States, Alette was evicted, with nothing but a note on the door and a few of her things left in the hall. Most of her possessions had been swiped by passersby. She called her girlfriend, who didn't answer. She called a friend next, asking to stay the night. They'd receive a settlement from the shop in France, but it would be quite a long time.

"I'm going back, and I'm staying there," she told Claire.

"Come home first," Claire said.

Claire had reopened the Athens shop with new determination. She stopped trying to get Alex to sign the divorce papers and, instead, had coffee with him on occasion. She'd settle into his familiar arms and kiss his familiar lips. She'd hide in his admiring gaze until a sort of sobering up occurred and she realized that their relationship couldn't move like this. Jasmine had been right that he had a place in her life, but it would take some time to figure out what that place was.

Jasmine's old neighborhood was healing, Marc told them as he smiled at Claire, then Alette. They Zoomed weekly, sharing news and worries, rekindling a sort of family tradition. Jasmine had always insisted on regular calls. "Family is all that sustains, no matter what." Marc assured the sisters that Nice's slow heartbeat had been kept rhythmic with donations and global assurances, the brilliant spirit of its citizens. The shop, surprisingly, was salvageable, and donations, along with insurance, would likely cover repairs.

"It could be nicer than ever before," he said. "If…"

When Alette, unhinged from her day-to-day, said, "I'm moving there. Can I stay with you, just for a month?" Marc didn't object. She watched the screen, looking for reservations in her sister's face, small creases in her forehead, but nothing came. And so she returned, imagining no dreamland. She envisioned a tough road. Her voice was more fixed than it'd ever been.

Jasmine's hometown was not ravaged but bruised and healing, and the shop stood sturdier than before, with Marc having already overseen some of the rebuilding. He showed Alette around with his phone, sent her estimates and bills, ideas for redesigning the place.

A month before leaving, Alette helped her sister on a busy Sunday. They prepared for the small crowd in Athens, an increasing number of regulars who would collect outside the door before they opened. Their mother's instructions lined the walls in framed print, her letters a collage that would be replicated in Nice. They cleaned and set up the tables and counter. They shared visions of the sister shop in Nice, which would no longer be a scorched or injured thing, but a dream, realized.

At one time, the sisters played a game that drove Jasmine crazy. They'd close their eyes, begin at the front door, and feel their way around the small home until they'd ventured to all rooms without a peek. The game would sometimes scare one or the other, a misstep would send electricity through their bellies, but they never cheated. Alette would reach out for her sister's hand.

They folded dough and eyed wax paper lined with their homemade truffles, prepared to instruction. They baked cookies and scones, mixed batters, and blasted French pop music as customers, one by one, began to line up in anticipation. The smells of fresh breads and sweet creams, of chocolate eclairs and almond macaroons, enveloped the sisters. They tied their aprons. Claire flipped the sign and unlocked the door.

RUNNING TOWARD THE SUN

Forty-five was steady, centered on a broad back just ahead of Owen. The man kept a respectable pace, the edges of his number plate fluttering around tiny safety pins. The combination of humidity and smog slowed the overall pack, and a few people were bowing out or stopping to walk mid-race. Owen refused. He even jogged in place at the water station as he downed the contents of a recycled paper cone.

The heavy-breathing mass of runners labored forward, creating a hypnotic soundtrack to accompany the blur of neon colors and reflective strips. Accounting for each step, technology lived in their shoes and on their wrists. Meanwhile, nature was angry, squeezing them with the heat of her breath. Every third or fourth person wore a paper mask now, a notable increase since Owen's first race a few years earlier.

California's inhabitants were ill-equipped for the mold and rot that came with constant moisture, not to mention the frizzed hair and heavy clothes. Intent on catching forty-five, Owen crumpled and tossed the cone as he picked up his knees to reach a good clip again. He resolved to pass the man within the next mile.

This is how Owen ran, with a clear focus on a person or landmark, then a surge. This is how he tried to live, but there was never anything so steady about his life as to focus the eyes long enough. Running was where Owen could meet goals, find some semblance of control.

The race was devoid of conversation for a time, uninterrupted by yells of support from spectators. The silence allowed Owen's mind to wander. He didn't want to entertain thoughts of home, but they kept arriving. His wife, Harper, who was either worrying over the endless spreadsheets that she kept at tax time or entertaining another man, would soon be served papers. She had no place in his mind right now.

He made a gesture as though waving off a fly, but he couldn't shake her image, her curly hair and oval face, the perfect heart mouth that pursed when she was attempting a joke. He ran faster, as though he could outrun his thoughts. He'd caught Harper cheating four times in three years, ever since she was diagnosed and successfully treated for breast cancer. The first time, he forgave her infidelity. He forgave her wholeheartedly. But by the third time, almost a year in remission, she might as well have been straddling some guy every day, every hour.

Two quick inhales through the nose, one exhale through the mouth. It was a breathing style he'd learned in cross-country as a kid, one that stung a little now. He found the man and tried to regain focus, but couldn't stop imagining that forty-five was one of Harper's lovers, one of the passing strangers who cared nothing about the fact that they'd clocked fifteen years as a married couple.

Owen sped up, surging prematurely to pass the broad-shouldered man with an almost aggressive closeness. He surged beyond four more people and found a place behind the number three.

He'd exhausted his breath, but had to push on. He focused again.

Three meant the woman must have signed up on the first day. She must be serious. She could be one of the leading women, perhaps *the* leading woman in the race. Over the last few races, Owen had placed among the leading women, a fact he took pride in. Not long ago, he could barely finish a few miles. For a while, Harper thought it funny to cup his belly and ask when he was expecting to deliver. It was an odd joke, seeing as how they'd tried for years – like most couples in the area – to no avail.

Barely flittering due to the woman's smooth stride, three was lower on the back, so Owen watched her hair swing instead, a pendulum. It was a way to watch time as he cut through it. He glanced at his watch, just as a resounding screech filled his ears. It wasn't coming from an animal, at least no animal Owen knew. The volume caused the entire pack to look up, then to the side. It sounded as though a large hinge were opening in the sky, but the sky itself remained still and heavy, a clouded periwinkle. The melted beauty of toxicity.

A few of the runners looked toward each other, shrugging. Owen kept his eyes on the woman's hair.

"Hey, I think I know you," a man said. He fell in line with Owen and matched his stride almost exactly. It was annoying, breaking Owen's concentration to pieces. The man wore a mask, but he slid it below his chin to speak.

"Oh yeah?" Owen said, trying to examine the man without breaking stride. He was a redhead, tall, with skin like egg shell, and a busy, freckled face. His smile seemed as easy as his stride. Meanwhile, Owen was beginning to feel the labor of each step.

"Joe Harding. You know Kate O'Brien, right?" He was speaking steadily, too, as though out for a stroll.

The masks do help, Owen thought, but he still had reservations. There had been studies that a person could build a certain immunity that would be beneficial in the coming years, and he had been one of many to hold out. Meanwhile, Owen released his words like balloons, gasping slightly after each one. "No." He stopped himself short of adding, "Think you got the wrong guy."

A strong wind pushed the heavy air against them, and Owen looked over. He noticed the man's eyes were like glass. Owen had dark hair, yet to gray, thick eyebrows – one of which drooped and bunched as though in perpetual deliberation, and his eyes were dull light-gray discs that only held depth in certain light.

"You sure? I swear I've seen you."

Owen specialized in estate law, and he rarely took on anything different. He had routines that required devotion. He didn't meet new people who weren't clients. He tried to keep focus on moving ahead, as what he couldn't control perpetually rattled him. He was pretty sure that if he'd met this guy or someone named O'Brien, he'd remember. "Maybe…I don't think so though."

The odd sound arrived again, only this time it was closer and accompanied by something heavier, a breaking noise. It was as though a machine were heading toward them.

"Sounds like someone needs to work on their car," Joe said dismissively. "So, O'Brien, she's friends with my wife." He gestured to his shirt, where there was a sticker with a pink ribbon and a muscular arm flexing beneath it. Men Run Pink was a solid running group, always placing in the first through fifth categories. The organization raised money for breast and reproductive cancer research by promising fast times, offering showy finish line moves, or by wearing survivors' names painted on the tops of their heads. One year, they were on Channel 4, promising to get face tattoos if they didn't meet goals. They were men who did this because they could. It was a good thing, a giving and wonderful, if grandstanding, thing.

"Sorry to hear," Owen said. "Your wife has breast cancer?" Asking someone what cancer they'd last been treated for was becoming common. *Which hospital?* was almost as common as *Where'd you go to college?*

"Ovarian. You?"

"My wife. Breast. Remission."

"That's good, man. You?"

"None. Nothing," Owen said.

"Nothing at all?" Joe was silent for a few strides, then said, "That's really great. I've had ten moles removed. I get checked monthly, a lot of close calls. Hey, a bunch of us are heading to the bar on 5th. Beer refuel around sunset when everyone's done and the air clears. Swing by! O'Brien might be there."

Joe pushed forward just as Owen was about to repeat the fact that he really didn't think he knew this O'Brien person, but Joe was fast – snaking through bodies seamlessly until he was out of sight. Owen entertained the idea of racing him. He tried to pick up his pace, knowing better, but just as he increased momentum, the humidity caused his lungs to swell. Instead, he slowed. The ponytail disappeared, and another woman passed.

The sound shifted then, and Owen felt as though the ground had cracked in half. Intense vibrations seemed to encapsulate him, beginning beneath his feet and soon pushing down at the same time. He watched, confused, as the new bank building in front of them leaned over, then began to crumble to the ground. A brief pause, and a mass of materials and dust released with force. It was too fast for them to react.

The woman in front of him was no longer upright. She had fallen to the ground and was now folding into herself, a piece of glass lodged into her leg near the ankle. Thick dust swirled around in the heavy air, obstructing Owen's line of sight.

He stopped running, but ended up knocking into something forcefully, tumbling over someone ahead. His attempt to pull back against gravity only made his body twist more. Another, taller man knocked into them both, and soon there was a pile of bodies, the slight woman still in his view, holding her leg, and Owen watched from the ground as a man yelled out for people to stop, go back the other way.

The bank building on 26th was collapsing, and building materials were now falling to the ground in chunks. There had been no explosion. It seemed the building was just giving out, giving up. Owen thought about doing the same.

Fire alarms began to sound, drowned out only by the noise of the crowd, the murmuring, the collective, "What do we do?" There was nothing but pained expressions. The street blanketed in mangled bodies, some of which wouldn't move again beneath the debris.

When he was eight, Owen used to watch his father at the museum. He never paid much attention to the art. It was always Tuesday evenings, and Owen's father would sit in front of the paintings with the brightest colors – watching them the way Owen watched cartoons. It was there, as he sat on the bench at the museum, elbows to knees, that Owen's father predicted the end of the world.

"I won't be around, but you sure will," he'd said. He'd said it often. Sometimes Owen would have to call his mother to ask that she come get them. Entering a sort of coma, his father would refuse to move. Entering, instead, the world of the art in front of him.

Owen closed his eyes and, for what seemed an eternity, didn't move. Until he awoke, he remained in the past, aware that time wasn't moving in his dream. He saw his father's face.

Some of the runners, those who led the pack, were close to the finish and, unknowing, sprinting at the announcement that the race would be shutting down behind them. Nothing had been explained. Leaning into the finish with flourish, people were breaking records. Best times were made a few miles ahead – at the same time, a young woman was lifted up by medics then placed on a gurney.

Owen tried to get up with the help of a stranger, but his head felt glued to the ground. There was a wetness pooling around him. There was a sharpness directly beneath him. He felt around and realized he'd landed where there was a crack in the blacktop; a jagged angle or rock had greeted his head on impact, and he imagined he now had a giant hole there, just above the ear. He imagined the street was lodged inside his head, and if they removed him, his life-force would gush out.

Two large hands stole him from his romantic notions. They gripped beneath his armpits and pulled him up. Realizing he was only stunned and a little dizzy, he stood on shaky legs. He saw a man twenty years younger than himself, slightly overweight, a man who was likely running his first marathon, trapped beneath a large metal rod. His leg looked as if it was severed through.

Owen felt around his head; he had a small bump forming, a little bleeding, but he was fine. He felt fine physically, anyway. Something inside had shifted. He offered to help in whatever way he could, moving in to join the crowd, but police were asking everyone to clear out, to find safer ground. The area was being blocked off quickly, efficiently, and there was only confused chatter about the collapse. A volunteer offered to drive him home or to a hospital.

Owen looked around. "Do we know what happened?"

"We're shutting everything down. We think the building collapsed; no one official thinks it was terrorism, but everyone on the ground thinks it is. The engineering might have just been – shitty." The volunteer locked eyes with Owen. He was no more than seventeen, had probably been helping out because a friend or family member had cancer.

"Thanks, kid. You need to be safe, too," Owen said. "And thanks to you," he called out to the man who had lifted him up. He saw the Men Run Pink insignia on the back of his shirt as the man bent over someone else to assist. Owen was dizzy but could walk a straight line. He tried to shake his head, shake back the equilibrium.

He drifted through a sea of people who were taking pictures of the disaster or rushing off. Most were being forced off by the increasing number of police and firefighters. Dust clouds rose up like hurdles. Waving his hands wildly in front of him as he walked, he tried to avoid them.

Owen sat at the bar, watching the news, wondering what kind of beer the Men Run Pink went for. Probably craft beers, IPAs or OPAs. Owen rarely drank, but when he did it was the cheap stuff, whatever was on special or marked *light* on the tap. He was sure none of them would show, but the thought of going home made his teeth itch.

Owen was still in his race gear, cell at his hip, and Harper had yet to call or text. In all fairness, she could be in therapy. She'd been going for two-hour sessions since the last indiscretion with a guy she worked with and had to see daily. She had gone, he thought, more than likely because her sex addiction was now inconveniencing *her* in practical ways.

"I saw that craziness on the news," the bartender said, pointing to Owen's number and placing a small brown napkin in front of him. The man was balding and overweight but had the rosy color of health, a thing that was becoming less common in the States.

Owen had been his weight around the time Harper started cheating. Now he had the sort of definition that made him understand why men at the gym flexed in front of the mirror. It was about reaching certain markers – looking for the nuance in definition, the sculpting of self.

"What are they saying?" Owen asked.

"Everything. Nothing. Hey, so long as you're not getting top shelf, it's on the house," he said. "I can rewind with this thing, I think. Play it back." He looked for the footage of the building, and stopped at a clip where everything was still intact. The sound was different over the footage, but Owen's stomach whirled as the building crumbled. A sea of runners scattered, and Owen could see himself, or someone else, falling over. Every second of the disaster had been captured, every angle.

Owen pointed to a beer on tap.

"So you think it was terrorism? I know what they're saying, but how can we discount it?" the bartender said, sliding over a cheap light beer and a small bowl of pretzels, as Owen glanced at his phone.

"Someone said it was a structural engineering problem, a foundation problem. Something like that," Owen said, unable to remember exactly who told him that.

"Yeah, right." the man said. "Likely."

There were images of bicycles all over the wall, in place of what would ordinarily be swathed in football or baseball paraphernalia. Most of them were paintings, a few photographs. One of the bicycles looked almost exactly like one Owen had as a child. He saw orange lights in his peripheral vision, and he blinked a few times to focus on the green paint with gold flecks, the thick handlebars and low seat. He stared at the bike as he munched handfuls of the tiny pretzels – remembering what it was like to ride as a kid – the freedom, the air smashing into his face as he took a sharp turn.

"Damn, man!" Joe said, placing a palm on Owen's back. "I sure didn't think you'd be here after that craziness."

"No better day to drink a beer," Owen said, looking up at Joe and another man, both in dark jeans and sport coats.

"What fresh hell, right? My buddy Dave, here, saw it all." Owen examined the man – looked to his hands – remembered the feeling of being lifted up like a child.

"Thanks," Owen said, unsure if he'd have to say more. The man nodded.

"Let's buy your next beer. On us," Joe said to the man behind the bar, handing him a black credit card. "My wife doesn't even know yet. She's knocked out – big week for her, and she's been doing a lot of serious sleeping. I think she could be competitive." He smiled.

Owen's father used to say that paintings were capable of coming to life, if you just knew how to look at them. He said they told him things. He thought the same of the television, the patterns in upholsteries. He believed radio waves were a portal to a better world, and he could hear the speakers' directives when they weren't on. If he were still alive, Owen thought, technology would have eaten him alive.

"You okay, man?" Joe said.

Owen tightened his eyelids, then opened his eyes again. The bike wheel had stopped moving, but the shadowy man in the background of the image was putting his hands up. The sky turned to bricks that began to fall, bending the wheels, sending chips of paint flying. The man, whose face emerged from the shadows, looked out at Owen with a sort of desperation in his eyes.

"I might've hit my head harder than I thought," Owen said, trying to dismiss the idea that his father was inside the painting. "I'll down this last beer, then head out."

Joe's friend placed a hand on the bar as he sat down. "Darrel," he said, then ordered a vodka and soda. "Your wife know yet?" he asked.

Owen followed Darrel's eyes to his ring. It wouldn't be long before the tan line would be all that was left to tell, and, eventually, that too would fade. "Fuck her," he said, surprising himself.

"Got it. Been there. Seems we all have. Well, all of us but Joe. His wife's perfect." Joe blushed, a thing redheads couldn't hide. "He married a fucking princess," Darrel added.

"She's special, that's for sure. But, then again, so am I," Joe said with a half-smile. He took the seat on the other side of Owen. "So, what happened, man? I still can't believe you're here. You have debris in your hood, man." Before Owen could answer, a woman with dark hair ran up to the guys and gave each of them a half-hug.

She nodded at Owen and said, "Hi! Do I know you?"

There were two channels on at the bar, both running footage of the race again and again. The collapse again and again. When one displayed close-ups of Owen's face, two more people bought him drinks. When another showed the same shot from a different angle, a round of shots arrived. The footage of him falling was shown, with the caption "Fourteen dead, three-hundred injured."

"Holy shit," Joe said, pointing at Owen's fall. Joe had been waving off drinks all evening, nursing a single beer, as Owen usually did.

Having lost track of the unsolicited alcohol he'd consumed, Owen found himself holding Kelly around the waist to help her guide a shot. They were playing pool, and he wasn't entirely sure when they'd moved from the bar. He felt as though he had died, or part of him had. Perhaps just the sober part.

"I think it's time for me to go," he said, pulling his hands from the woman's waist. Owen felt his stomach twisting and ran out of the bar; as soon as he hit the dense air, he heaved. He ran to his car, but Joe came up behind him and swiped his keys, said something about the hospital. Joe grabbed his arm tight. Pulled him back.

"I'm driving you. Darrel will follow."

Joe looked over every few minutes as he navigated Owen's Honda as best he could to the drunken and circuitous directives. Darrel and Kelly followed behind them. There was no car in the driveway when they arrived, no texts or missed calls on Owen's phone. There was no way Harper was still in therapy, and she never worked late.

Owen took care to remove his windbreaker before trying the lock. He waved Joe and Darrel off, yelling his thanks as they pulled away in Darrel's Jeep. When the key didn't seem to work, he tried again. Again. He walked around to the window and peered inside.

He made out the living room, a rich blue and brown room, complete with a two-person couch and bright orange throw pillows, a flat screen, a fireplace – all the things he dreamed about owning as a child who grew up in a cramped apartment. He imagined himself a newlywed, his wife straddling him on the matching chair. But as soon as the image arrived, it morphed. She was straddling some other man – any man – on that same chair.

Love was lodged beneath his ribs, a painful thing. A thing that wanted to push itself to the surface, break through his skin. Owen smashed the window with his fist. His hand bled, but he felt nothing. He stepped onto the fluffy carpet, eased off his shoes, looked around. There were no lights on, no wife, no nothing. He was alone and bleeding. He grabbed a towel from the kitchen and stretched out on the couch.

The materials used to construct the bank building, which were supposed to be more efficient and environmentally friendly, were officially to blame, according to the media. The building had collapsed due to too low a resistance, and it wasn't helped by the constant atmospheric pressure.

"I can't explain it," an architect being interviewed on TV was saying. He paused for a calculated moment. "The humidity has been off the charts. We tested for extreme scenarios, conditions." Owen smelled detergents and metal. He realized he was no longer at home.

His hand was bandaged. Harper was there, her soft mouth smiling gently at his open eyes. "You remember yesterday?" she asked, quizzing him. "Do you remember a man named Joe driving you home? Breaking the window?"

"I remember you weren't there," he said, looking up at the TV, narrowing his eyes so the picture stopped jumping around.

The architect's name was long and blurry at the bottom of the screen. Owen blinked a few times before the screenshot shifted to the building's owner, a real estate tycoon who was blatantly unapologetic. The man explained that the real problem was the fault of the manufacturers who hadn't done adequate testing themselves. He said something about outsourcing, which made no sense at all.

"The building was built with green technology. It was truly a remarkable feat. We had solar panels and all recycled steel beams. We used a concrete mix for the walls to maintain temperatures but were diligent about sourcing. Those manufacturers should have done due diligence as well!" He raised his fist. "*They* should've tested durability in an unpredictable climate, and I will be sure to never do business with faulty manufacturers again." The split screen showed the architect cringe, as though unsure if he was included in the shot.

As the building owner continued to speak, Owen began to see flashes of orange light. He closed his eyes and saw the race, the number forty-five. He would pass this guy within the next mile, he thought. It was the echo of a thought. He heard the creaking of a collapsing building, eyed Joe. His hand had grazed a woman's hip at a bar, and there was no vindication, no sensation at all.

The lights continued to flash as though projected on the backs of his eyelids. "Where were you?" he asked. Harper would soon be receiving his divorce papers, he reminded himself. It had been in the works for years, but he was ready now. He just had to give the final go-ahead.

"An appointment, sweetheart. I told you –"

He reached out to his side and felt his wife's hand warm his own. He saw Joe's smile in his mind – discussing his wife as though she were a precious person to be revered and honored. He imagined the light pink lips parting slowly, the freckles bunching at his cheeks. He squeezed his wife's hand a little too hard, and she pulled back.

In his reverie, Owen saw himself running faster, surging ahead at top speed, passing the regulars, the die-hards. He saw himself catching up and surpassing, crossing the finish line to cheers and a buzz of his watch that celebrated his best time. His arms up in a V, he'd make one change at a time.

His first goal was clarity. "I'm leaving you," he whispered.

Harper rested her head on his belly as he reached the first marker in his mind. She said, "My cancer's back."

The MRI machine was huge, a coffin filled with radio waves, portals to other worlds. The unseen force pulsed through Owen's body.

Owen's father used to say that the only way we survive as things get harder in the world is to take long periods of rest, to hibernate like cicadas. "Go deep," he'd say, before sending Owen to his room for entire weekends. Owen would be happy to do so, to avoid watching his father's eyes bug out when he believed he was melting into the carpet or being sucked into the television.

Owen had been a teenager before he understood his father's illness for what it was. For most of his childhood, Owen had been convinced it was his inadequacy that kept his father distant, that fed his odd behavior.

"The earth is like a vice, squeezing slightly more each day," his father said.

Upon release, the doctor gave both Owen and Harper masks. "Whenever an immune system is compromised, we insist. The air can break the respiratory system down faster when you are unwell." He wore a white coat, a traditional doctor's coat. Owen thanked him.

"Is it normal, what's going on with me? Do you think something could've been loosened in my mind? My father was – "

The look on the doctor's face seemed to tell Owen that this *Am I crazy?* question was not unique. "If the visions continue, it might be a good idea to follow up with a psychiatrist, but give yourself some time."

Some months passed, and Owen's hallucinations were gone. He hadn't divorced. Harper had rounds of treatment, and he sat in the chair next to her while imagining that Joe and his wife were a few floors above. He wore his mask every time he left the house. The safety that the masks provided was addictive. So much so, it was becoming rare to see someone without a mask.

Harper fought, and follow-up appointments revealed she was in the clear again, but she was to remain indoors at all times.

The relentless humidity compounded the air's venom. It felt as though a moldy washcloth was draped around Owen every time he went outside to jog, so he stopped. The use of inhalers had tripled, and the constant pressure in the air kept people indoors where they blasted their fans and air conditioners so much so that brown-outs were occurring on the north and east sides of town. The toxic air led to fewer races in the area and larger mosquitos.

Other structural issues were occurring as well, fissures and threats, though nothing as drastic as the bank building collapse. Not yet. Some said it was coincidence, some still clung to the idea of terrorism, and no one believed the tycoon. Not anymore.

Owen spent his days ignoring calls from other lawyers who offered him shares in mass lawsuits, calls which seemed to increase in quantity daily. He ran on a treadmill in the basement after work. He ran fast, as though, if he could reach a certain speed, he'd be able to find something new.

He was really picking up his knees, focusing on the numbers leading to his goal: six miles. Once the tally hit six, he'd move to the elliptical. He zoned out, listening to Prince on his phone and, pushing forward, thinking here and there about whether he'd make a smoothie after his workout, or stop by the vegetarian restaurant and pick up a tofu breakfast sandwich.

The buzzing interrupted this thought. Owen looked down to find a text from an unidentifiable number.

"Want to get a drink, buddy?" it read. "But just one or two," the next text said. Suddenly, Owen felt as though he were racing downhill. He clicked the arrow down at four miles and two kilometers. He texted, carefully.

"Sure. Same place?"

When he went upstairs to grab a water, Harper beamed. "Got you a breakfast sandwich from Green Cuisine." Her saccharine demeanor might have been the result of the potential lawsuits. She believed they would soon be rich.

"Thank you," he said, realizing that what he really wanted was the smoothie.

Joe was there when Owen arrived, a mask upturned on the bar in front of him. He was sitting directly beneath the image of the bicycle, which looked ordinary tonight. Owen was well-dressed. His belt and shoes, a camel color, matched; a thing Harper had always insisted on when they went out, a thing he never thought of on his own.

"You drink the cheap shit, right, man?" Joe asked.

"It's on me," Owen said.

"I know it's kind of strange I contacted you out of the blue. It's just – I feel like that day we met – "

"Thanks for looking out for me that day."

"Of course, man. I feel like we've been to war together. That's why I called. They're still talking about it as being a tipping point. The day the first building crashed."

"A tipping point," Owen repeated, watching the bicycle closely, waiting.

"I wasn't even injured like you, and I keep getting these visions, like everything is going to crumble around us," Joe said.

Owen thought about his father and became desperate to shift the conversation. "How's your wife?"

Joe smiled at the bartender, a young woman who didn't pour out the foam. "I think you need to flush the tap," he said. His eyes locked on

Owen's then, and he spoke slowly, deliberately: "She was great. Just another ordinary treatment. Then a few days outside in this toxic air, and it's back." He looked down at Owen's ring. "It's an odd world, Owen. All I do now is go to that hospital and come home. She's all I see, and she's fading. She's still funny and lovely and perfect. She's still my soft place to land. But she's dying, and I feel like I'm already alone. I don't know why I'm telling you this."

"I get it," Owen said. He realized the beer tasted off, a bit too bitter. He sipped it, nodding.

"I wonder if I feel like the entire world is crumbling around us because it is, or because my wife is dying."

"The world is condensing," Owen said, repeating his father's words without realizing.

"It's this humidity," the bartender said, laughing, then rushed off to help someone else.

"I wanted to tell you that day," Joe began.

"Tell me what?" Owen looked up at the bike, then closed his eyes. He saw Harper on the couch as he listened to Joe's confession – how he'd met her at a bar, how he thought if he hooked Owen up with Kelly, it would be even. He was so sorry, to his wife, to Owen…he'd wanted to make things right. He saw Owen that day, and he thought he could make things right.

"I even thought of confessing that day, but then all this – "

After years of underground hibernation, cicadas emerge to sing during the hottest part of the day, clattering on and ingesting water-rich sap that they then sweat out, much like a runner would.

Harper could no longer lie to him. No one could. The masks everyone wore now, even indoors, made them more honest. It reminded him they were all dying, and there could be no guilt. Everyone had to look everyone else in the eye. Owen, ready for whatever was to come, set goals, set sights, and moved beyond them. Harper's papers would be served, officially, a few months before his final race. They would divorce, but he would not leave her.

He felt the rhythm of his stride effortless as he trained. Owen, racing himself in his apartment, which was pretty much a gym with a bed now that he was single, good at being alone. He coped. He kept air conditioning blasting. He wore out two treadmills from what seemed overuse. They'd get hot and stop moving, then sparked. He ran every time he wanted something to change. The air had held people in place, forced them to stop moving forward, but now the pressure was beginning to release, and the city hosted a 5K.

The day of his last race, when the starter gun sounded, Owen's adrenaline took over. He wore the Men Run Pink pin, having signed up online as a donor after Joe texted him. His wife had passed.

Because Owen was part of the effort, he would be timed. A sensor tied to his shoelace beeped when he hit mile markers. There was no one to settle in behind, no one to race. In fact, when Owen set out from the start, he realized that all those around him were falling behind quickly. Owen was one of only a few at the start with just a mask. Most ran virtually from their treadmills at home. They were projected on big screens, their times clicking away. Owen ran and ran, seeing Joe at one point on the screen, powering forward without moving from his living room. Owen had real miles to run, and he was glad for them.

Medics drove alongside the small heat of runners, the twenty or so die-hards who were in this last race in top form. Owen led them but wished someone would pass him so that he had something to target. He counted steps, focused on landmarks, but they would become blurry in his view. A window could blow out, the concrete below his feet could split. Owen would simply cut through the air as though it were heavy fabric.

Other runners labored behind him, and many were stopping, some falling. Meanwhile, Owen ran in such a way that each step echoed. He imagined his footfall could be felt eight feet below where the cicadas burrowed and settled as nymphs. He crushed the ground beneath him, lifting his arms in a V at the finish, locking eyes with the camera that greeted him in such a way that he swore he could see beyond its lens to the world that was waiting.

DON'T TEASE THE ELEPHANTS

The Jeep was perfect for safari because it didn't have zippers. It had real windows, up-and-down windows. The guy who stood in the little hut, who took Rattle's money, told us that because we had the right kind of Jeep, we qualified for the good part. Being here made me want to go to the real jungle, but I was a kid who had to take what I was given. That's what Mom said anyway.

We already passed the part where we could get real close to the animals. The deer and those other things that look like deer but shorter, with horns, came to the window and ate granola out of my hand. They had big teeth like a kid I know who gets made fun of for having big teeth, and when they ate the granola, it tickled my palm. Then we got to the windows-up part. When I saw my first elephant, I got scared and reached for Mom like I was still a little kid or something. It looked right at me, and it was as big as the Jeep.

Mom had on that green sweater that was always falling off her shoulder. My hand accidentally hit her belly, and she jerked back, adjusting her sweater so the strap part wasn't showing. Mom doesn't like people touching her belly since she got it tucked, so I said *sorry*. I felt dumb after, real dumb. I was reaching for her hand like a little kid or something. Mom's boyfriend, who was called Rattle because he used to catch rattlesnakes for a living, was there, and I was glad he was on his phone and didn't see the babyish thing I just did.

"Dinosaurs!" my brother said. My brother is a baby. Babies can be pretty dumb.

"No. That's an elephant," I told him. "Get with it."

Mom and Rattle both laughed. They always laughed when I told Cody to *get with it*, so I told him that a lot. He did need to get with it, thinking an elephant was a dinosaur.

Rattle knew about all animals, and I wanted to ask him about the elephants, but he was still on his phone, and adults don't like being interrupted when they're on their phones.

"Hey, Mom, can we take pictures of them? I want to show Joey that I saw an actual elephant," I said.

"No camera, sweetie. Unless Rattle stops whatever he's doing for two seconds and takes a picture with his phone." Rattle looked up at her, then he looked at me. His brown hair was long, wavy. He had a beard like I will grow when I'm older. I have to get my hair cut real short, close to my skull so that Mom doesn't have to take me all the time. And my hair is blond, not brown like I always wished it was, but I knew there was no point in complaining.

"You want a picture of that one, kid?" he asked me, pointing to the biggest elephant.

"I guess." I watched as he pushed a few more buttons on his phone, then aimed the little camera.

"Dinosaur," my kid brother said, but this time we all ignored him.

"I want to work here," I said, carefully. "I want to be a bouncer here."

"A bouncer!" Mom laughed and, as she did, that sweater fell down again, and she pulled it up.

I looked to Rattle who wasn't laughing because he knew how big a deal it was for a man to decide his profession. He was a bouncer at a nightclub, which is a pretty dangerous job. Not as dangerous as catching rattlesnakes, probably, but pretty dangerous.

Mom dated a lot, and Rattle was the first guy I liked. Most of the guys she picked smelled bad, the way my real dad used to smell, and my real dad was mean. Rattle smelled fancy, like the mall. Even when he drank beer, he didn't smell like the beer.

"You know, kid, I bet those elephants could use a bouncer. Some people don't know how to act around animals."

"That's what I'm saying. See, Mom? Rattle knows."

"I don't know where he gets these things," she said about me, while I was right there, and laughed like I wasn't right there, which I hate.

"Yeah," I said to Rattle. I ignored Mom the way she was ignoring me. She put my brother on her lap, and he started pointing to the zebra on the other side, way down near the trees. The zebra just looked like painted deer to me, so I kept on about the elephants. "See, I'll keep the bad people away, the people who try to do dumb stuff like ride the elephants."

Rattle nodded. He said, "I'll tell you a story, kid. One sec." He began typing something else into his phone. Mom cut her eyes at him the way she did me when she caught me stealing extra chocolate milk after bedtime. Chocolate milk keeps me awake and feeling full, but it's so good! I got sick off the stuff once and puked it up for a whole fifteen minutes, but when I was done, I just wanted more chocolate milk. That's how good that stuff is.

"Who are you texting?" she asked. Rattle ignored her the way she ignored me, and everyone ignored my little brother who was now sticking his tongue on the window.

Rattle looked up. "You know what people do?" he asked me.

I shrugged. I had kind of forgotten the conversation because I was thinking about chocolate milk, but when I looked out the window and saw that big, hulking elephant, I remembered. "What?"

"People tease them and poke at them. An elephant would need a really brave bouncer, someone he trusts, because elephants can get mad and hurt people. Even the wrong people." He went back to his text.

"That's it!" Mom said to him. "I am not the one to put up with this."

I wished she'd quit yelling. I didn't like it when she got like this. When she got like this with Dad, he threw stuff and yelled back. It went on forever. But Rattle just put his phone away and looked at me like he was about to tell a ghost story. He told good ghost stories.

"One elephant, a few years back, became so angry at a guy that he speared the man with his giant tusks and threw him up in the air." He looked up like he saw it happening. "Then, when the man

89

landed, that elephant held a giant foot over the man's head. The man screamed, and the elephant crushed his skull with one stomp. This was a circus elephant, so there were a lot of people around. Some of the people said that the guy's head made a popping sound like a giant piece of popcorn." He reached out for Mom's shoulder and started rubbing where the strappy part was. He whispered to her, "It's about work." And I asked if he thought an elephant bouncer's head would pop like that.

"No, kid, a good bouncer wouldn't get his head popped."

"Mom, what do you think? Really, no making fun. Would I make a good bouncer?" She gave me her real smile, the one where she shows her teeth. I took that to mean *yes*, and my fate was sealed.

"Why are elephants like that to people who aren't bouncers?" I asked.

"Well, the man had been teasing the elephant by offering him an apple, then pulling it back, so I guess the big guy got mad. Elephants are used to getting treated badly by people. People hunt them and take their tusks. When people are good to the elephants, though, the elephants are good back," Rattle explained.

"I'll be good to my elephant."

I saw Rattle take out his phone when it beeped again, and I could see a picture of a girl in one of those text bubbles. It was like she was a comic book character, and I almost asked if she was. I wanted to ask, but Mom didn't like it when he talked about other women. I asked her all the time if Rattle was going to stick around, and she'd always say, if he stopped talking with other women, he would. She told me to tell her when I saw him talk to other women, which I never had till now. But this was a comic book woman in a text bubble, so I didn't think that'd count.

I knew Rattle wouldn't stick around forever. No one did. But we were both in this Jeep right now, at safari, which was pretty cool. Besides, I knew to take what I got. As we approached the final part of the tour, I asked Rattle what he knew about lions.

"Kid, I'll tell you a story about lions."

I sat at attention as he put his phone back in his pocket. Whatever he was about to say, I knew I'd never forget it.

THE COUPLE ON THE ROOF

Anthony's wrapped knees bent to ease the wobbling. Everything about this simple chore felt complex. His lack of dexterity, the pain, the nagging desire to ease back down the ladder. He examined the tree and adjusted his feet, testing out his equilibrium. But just as he stretched out the tape measure to the thickest branch – the one that quivered threateningly near the bedroom window during storms – the ladder tilted, skidding along the ceramic-studded asphalt tiles.

It fell as Anthony reached out. He looked over his shoulder in time to make out the blur of his wife's taillights; he waved as she turned the corner with a screech.

His stomach, unaware of circumstance, churned audibly in anticipation of the celery and peanut butter he'd prepared himself as a reward for completing this task. Given all the trouble this was turning out to be, he decided he was due an actual peanut butter sandwich now, complete with lightly toasted nine-grain bread. Hold the celery.

He pivoted his feet out into a slightly wider stance as the ladder bounced off the bush. The metal taunted him with a clang, landing unevenly, slowly sinking into the pool. He was safe but, alas, stuck on the roof.

Georgia had instructed him, repeatedly, not to go up there whenever he brought it up because, apparently, she'd known better. He felt a sort of dumb vulnerability as he looked out at endless gray roofs and yellow-green or xeriscaped lawns.

Anthony had ignored his wife's warnings because he wanted to prove her wrong, and he knew he could do the job quickly if the branch wasn't too thick. Unfortunately for Anthony, he couldn't use the extra time productively, as the chainsaw was still on the bench by the garage. Georgia would've chuckled at this development.

His very position on this roof was the result of rebellion. Georgia dissuaded his every impulse lately. She told him not to do anything and to avoid everything, citing the many times his inclinations had led to unfortunate outcomes. If Georgia had her way, Anthony would be a fixture in the living room; he'd live for the sole purpose of hauling in groceries and preparing her nightly footbath before *The Voice* – then excuse himself as she watched, because, according to her, Anthony chewed too loudly and ruined the show.

And as much as Georgia wanted an inert husband, *she* was always on the go. She would be gone today for four hours – the duration of her shift at the craft boutique. Her part-time job was a new thing, an unnecessary thing because she'd been a lawyer for eighteen years and had earned more than enough for the both of them to live off of, if somewhat modestly by her tastes, for their remaining days. Anthony had contributed some, too, although he'd been something of a freelancer since the Marines, which meant dwindling savings as he aged. He had a small house he'd purchased with his first wife, Patricia, but it was a house that Georgia promptly sold to one of her old clients.

Anthony examined the clouds. Cirrus? Cumulus? Neither seemed quite right for these clouds, which appeared a worn-out comforter shielding the sky. He nodded stoically at his unfortunate timing. He felt like a character in one of those Griswold movies, only there were no endearingly irritating family members holed up in the house to rescue him or even check things out in case he fell. His body, he imagined, would land like a bag of sand on the thorny rose bushes below or roll into the pool as the ladder had. There was no heroic scene in which he'd dive successfully from roof to pool, especially not with the ladder crossways and slowly sinking.

The hiss and grumble of a motorcycle down the road set Anthony's sandwichless stomach on edge. He had been standing rather securely to this point, but now felt the grainy roof tiles moving along the bottoms of his sneakers. He repositioned his arms around the thick tree branch he'd hoped would be firewood by now, and hugged it tight, then positioned himself like a ballerina. His long and narrow feet created the V of first position that allowed him to squat some and relieve the pressure on his knees.

Anthony tried to visualize success. He imagined himself flipping off the house then landing like a cat. So many years had passed since he felt any semblance of control over his body, but his mind was elastic – so said his shrink. He felt a rush of adrenaline, then shifted to hear something in his knee pop.

Creaky and watchful, he scanned the perimeter. A neighbor would notice soon enough, he was sure. He saw a man on a Harley out in front of Josephine's place. The man hesitated to knock on the front door. It looked like the scene of a romance; the other man almost finally making that move, then backing away.

"Hey," Anthony yelled, but he could barely hear himself, and this guy was some ways down the street. Josephine's husband was no good. The guy was a drunkard, showing up on the front lawn naked and yelling, running after teenagers who looked at him the wrong way; he'd been seen threatening Josephine in public more than once. Anthony had even caught him pissing in Georgia's rose bushes once at 2 a.m., quietly grumbled at the guy, then explained that he should move on before his wife came out with a rifle.

Anthony wondered if he could manage a way to sit and tried hoisting himself onto the branch, but he couldn't get the momentum. He wanted to sit, but the roof was rather steep. The only way to balance would be a foot on either side of the apex, which would mean some uncomfortable sack shifting he didn't want to try out.

Anthony loosened one hand from the branch to pull up his circulation socks. They were thick black things that felt a little like torture in this triple-digit heat. He remembered a time when he thought old men wore thick black socks during summer in some solidary move of rebellion – a *fuck you* to all the summer fashions and young people with their fast-pumping blood. It wasn't until he turned seventy-three that he realized they were medicinal. Or at least physically helpful. He wondered why they always had to be black, though – not a good color for shorts.

A woman with a golden Lab shuffled by. She looked up briefly, barely registering Anthony before the Lab jerked her toward a squirrel. He didn't know the woman, figured she was one of the dozen or so who lived in the cheaper housing at the mouth of the neighborhood. Her workout clothes were mismatched, and the way she moved, it appeared her feet hurt. He called out to her.

"Hello," she said, and waved, then continued on.

"Shit," Anthony said, taking an awkward step. "HELLO!" he yelled. She waved again. "No, help – not hello. Help!"

Just as she looked back again, the Harley did a U-turn and raged past them, which drowned out Anthony's pleas. *No, go back and knock. That husband of hers is no good,* Anthony thought. Dragging the young lady along, the dog surged after the bike. Anthony imagined scaling down the wall toward the bush. He recalled himself in fatigues, crawling on the ground like a spider, unafraid of the world.

A tough wind, and he imagined falling instead.

The sun was fading the blue paint on the garage door. The sun was fading the grass, which was now almost hay, damp hay. The lawns and bleached pool bottoms in yard after yard seemed a calling card for the bland lives of Anthony's neighbors, most of whom he'd shared beers and Scrabble with at one point or another when Georgia was going through her *How to Win Friends and Influence People* stage. She didn't seem to care much anymore, but for a while she had a running list of all the people she'd picked to show up at her funeral. "I want you to keep a list, too, doll," she'd said to Anthony who knew his odds of outliving her were slim and didn't much care to keep lists of any sort.

It began to rain. Anthony didn't bother to yell after the young lady again as she picked up speed. He'd been stuck on the roof for almost an hour. His skin drank in the soft rain; he thanked the sky. Maybe he could use this time to think. He so rarely had quiet time. He'd read that meditation was something to master, despite pain or awkward positioning, so he tried it, but got distracted when he heard thunder.

Four houses down, he saw a little girl who was said to be something of a terror. She'd once jumped into the back of someone's pickup, which got that poor guy in quite a bit of unnecessary trouble — at least, according to neighborhood legend. He'd also heard that she sometimes broke into neighbors' homes just to expose their personal vulnerabilities, then left notes about how she'd done it and how they should rethink their security systems.

He remembered the girl sneaking extra handfuls of candy when Anthony and Georgia sat out on the porch in their worn skeleton costumes last Halloween. "That little punk!" Georgia said while the girl was still within earshot. They wore the same costumes each year, bought the same candy, but Anthony had made a mental note to get a little extra next year, just in case she came back. She was on the cusp of being too old to trick or treat.

"She's just a kid," he'd argued that night, smiling at the girl when she glanced back, and distracting his wife by offering to refill her rum and Coke.

Anthony squat-hovered like a sumo wrestler. He was extra thankful now for the foresight to wrap his knees that morning, but he wished he'd eaten the celery and peanut butter before he climbed up. He longed for Georgia to come home. And at the same time, he dreaded her return, which would likely come with taunting and ridicule.

The drizzle stopped, and the windy heat felt as though it were coming from a hair dryer. When the gold Cadillac finally turned the corner, he stood. Georgia's low-heeled shoes hit the drive, and he immediately felt the nerves dancing on his chest. He heard her calling his name, watched as she examined the ladder in the backyard. "Oh, Anthony. How sloppy!" she said, unaware of his position above her. She walked around, looked up. "And the damn tree branch is still there. What'd I tell him?" She couldn't see Anthony due to his location and the relative darkness, which camouflaged his leg so that it too looked like a tree branch. She called his name again. Again.

Anthony considered the ridiculous nature of hiding, and he worried all the more about her response. She'd think he was senile. Hell, maybe he was.

"Hey, she's mean, right?" a girl's voice said, a whisper. Anthony almost fell as he scrambled to turn around. He saw, on his neighbor's roof, the little terror with the curly hair and round glasses. She wore shiny pants with geometric shapes on them, green shoes, and a yellow striped shirt. Had it been daylight, she might have hurt his eyes, maybe even caused a stroke.

"Your parents let you climb?"

"Mom lets me do whatever. Now shhhh. She'll hear you, Mister."

"Anthony."

"Mister Anthony, we need to be quiet or we'll get in trouble."

"How'd you get up there?"

"Crawled up this gate thing."

"The trellis?"

"Yup. Mom calls me a monkey. I can climb anything. Mister Anthony, I don't want you to jump. I always liked you. When we see you at the grocery, you smile at me. *She* doesn't. Most kids get smiles. I don't."

"Sounds like you're working on a pretty healthy anxiety disorder there, little one. People probably smile at you all the time, but you're short, so you just don't see them." Anthony's right foot wouldn't move. It was numb to the point of sharp pain, and he still heard Georgia moving around in the house as she calling his name. Her voice was faint. "I need to get down from here, kid. You too. You think maybe you can prop that ladder up for me?"

"Oh sure! Watch how fast I can get down!" She rushed to climb down, and in doing so her bright sneaker skidded and flew off. The girl stumbled, and as she did, her other leg folded beneath her. Anthony watched the tiny body roll off the roof. He gasped, then yelled out.

"Anthony! What in God's name are you doing up there?" Georgia shrieked.

"The girl! That curly-headed girl crawled up on the Harrisons' roof. She just fell. Go get her!" Anthony didn't wait for the logical thing. He didn't ask his wife to pull the ladder up. Instead, he placed his long foot on the gutter and then angled his toes against the concrete bricks below. When he reached the windowsill, he jumped, once more a soldier, landing hard on a soft patch of mud. His knee cracked, but still seemed to function well enough when he stood. He was elastic.

"What in the hell did you do, Anthony? How do things like this always happen with you? Are you okay? Where is this girl? I didn't hear anything."

"She fell. She has to be here." Anthony looked behind the bushes and ran – for the first time in years – around the neighbor's backyard. He lifted the tarp on the pool and rushed around the side.

"Darling, perhaps I should take you in. Maybe you got delirious from being up on that roof. Were you up there the whole time I was gone? You were, weren't you? You were. There's no girl, darling. Come on in. We'll watch some television, and you can run me a footbath."

Just as she threw her thick gray hair back and sauntered inside, Anthony heard a whisper. He crouched down and peered into the darkness of a cluster of trees behind his neighbor's home. He saw the girl's bright sneakers and moved toward them.

"A monkey, remember?" she said, close to the ground as though in combat. "I can do anything." He smiled her way, hoping she'd see.

As Anthony ran the warm water from the tub, he realized that he hadn't finished the job. He grabbed his chainsaw from the garage and positioned the ladder once again. He didn't bother measuring this time, didn't ask permission; he just began to work at it as his wife dozed off intermittently, watching *The Voice*. His joints ached and screamed. He angled the blade, spun splinters out of the wood, allowed the branch to fall, and watched it plunk against the bushes. He returned inside, wife none the wiser, and chewed his peanut butter sandwich loudly, unabashedly, as Georgia watched her shows.

"Can you chew quieter? Goodness!" she said, waking from beneath a light blanket. She waited for a commercial, then turned off the jets in her footbath, removed two wrinkly feet and placed them on a towel gently, then spoke again. "That girl is no good, whoever she is. That is, if you really did see her. We might want to make an appointment with a therapist. We can call the VA."

"Georgia, I don't – "

"Hush. It's coming back on."

Anthony excused himself and walked out the door as Georgia's feet dried. He dumped the foot water on their struggling grass, upturned the bath, and left it on the porch. He felt the ground beneath him, soggy but solid. Anthony's feet had always been particularly long and narrow, tough to find shoes for, not ideal for dancing or balancing. But he used them that night.

He walked along the street until all the stiffness in his joints and ankles eased. He walked until the leaden feeling of his legs dissolved. He knew his wife was dozing again because she wasn't calling after him.

When Anthony's dreams terrorized him, Georgia would cradle his head. She'd stay up all night, stroking his arm from the shoulder, lightly, her touch like soft rain. He never opened his eyes, never let her see his appreciation. When he was wide awake the next day, he wouldn't think of night. She'd gripe about this and that, and he'd disagree inaudibly.

The day Anthony spent on the roof, the day he walked for hours into the night, he slept soundly for the first time in twenty years. In his dream, he saw the man he'd once been, and he ventured toward him. But then a Harley rushed beside him, and he gave its driver a head nod. A little girl in loud clothes danced on the sky – totally free. People moved all around him, and he smiled at them.

He began climbing onto his roof occasionally after that day if only to test his equilibrium here and there and get a touch closer to the sun. He began climbing onto the roof daily after a while. He ran footbaths and left the wife to her shows. He kept his eyes closed as the pads of her fingers traced the base of his neck some nights – when the nightmares surfaced.

Then the day came when he tried to sneak out, and she whisper-growled, "And just where do you think you're going?"

No one thing is all one way, Anthony said, positioning the ladder that night. He held tight and eased up after Georgia, ready in case she decided to back out. But Georgia went along, climbing in her pale green nightgown.

She wobbled on the roof at first, but scanned the neighborhood with intense interest, quiet appreciation. She said she remembered crawling out on her own roof as a girl, leaning back on her elbows and staring up at the sky with her sister, freestyle futures formulating on their tongues.

From their perch, the couple's view stretched out to eternity; Anthony and Georgia's fingers threaded and their gazes widened. The girl with curly hair sometimes biked by and waved without looking up. Others expressed concern, asked if the couple needed help. Some whispered that they must be insane.

"Just two old birds who found their perch," Anthony would say whenever people appeared worried. It became their daily rendezvous, no matter what.

Much would remain the same. Anthony's nightmares arrived less frequently, the imprint of events too deep a wrinkle in his brain to fully erase, and Georgia would continue to cradle his head. They would continue to bicker and gripe or offer passive-aggressive silences in exchange for sour words. Anthony would continue to run footbaths, and Georgia would watch *The Voice*.

But they'd always return to the roof where they were briefly a piece of the sky. They would sit up there until the time came to fly away.

THE INCONVENIENCE
OF IT ALL

I fold backward like a pack of matches, curl my head under my legs, and lift my hands toward the sky. This performance is the result of three hours of stretching daily, even on holidays, even when arthritis swells my joints. The judges examine me, body-to-face, calculating my age. They nod at #7, who stumbled no less than four times, and #12, who was stiff and botched the backflip.

I wait in the back row. I didn't mess up a thing, yet they deliberate as though I had real competition. When #7 is called to the front, I fight the urge to step forward. I want to shove her out of the way and claim my rightful space.

"The back row is excused," says a slender judge. He wears a black turtleneck and fitted slacks. His voice is as slippery as glass.

I sit in the back seat and watch a smattering of raindrops fall. There are two other performers on the ride. We, the unchosen. Melinda, twenty-seven and gorgeous, is in the passenger seat. And Gio, nearing thirty-five and flirtatious – who said I had nice toes on the way up to the audition – is next to me, with his head tilted against the opposite window. We are all staring out our respective windows, in fact, settling into the deep quiet of rejection. The rain begins to race around the car's exterior. The driver silently curses the wet roads and sloppy turns. His gruff tone, in some inexplicable way, feels close to my heart.

I do not say goodbye as Gio collects his backpack and eases out with umbrella poised, and I do not wave when Melinda gets off a few blocks later and runs by my window. I live the farthest south, the least desirable area of Canton, but today this doesn't bother me. Today, it feels fitting, just like my teal tights and this rain, and what I think is the start of a mean case of heartburn.

"Aging is highly inconvenient," I tell the driver.

"Yep," he says.

I told my landlord the same thing last week when he asked why the rent was late again. He told me to get a new job, one that's more suitable. Let me tell you, I would've plucked his toupee and thrown it in a puddle had he said that today. But, here I sit. Maybe he's right. I always take this ride. The Gios and Melindas of the world only take it every now and again.

Before her coronary event, Coach used to look deep into my eyes and tell me that I can and will make it. She'd tell me again and again. I place my hand to my heart. I repeat her mantra as the shuttle slides on a flooded portion of Morse Road. "I can and I will."

"Huh?" the driver says. I ignore him. I have to get my mind right.

I think about a YouTube video that my neighbor showed me last week. It was a contortionist who had gone viral, and there was nothing remarkable about her performance.

I stretch out my hips, balance my ankle on the opposite knee, bend deeply until I can kiss my thigh, then move my head beyond it. I ease my leg back further so that my calf is situated like a travel pillow. I'll work on my flips. If I can come up with a routine, maybe my old signature routine, and add a backflip at the end, I'll go viral for sure. For once in a long time, my age could be an attribute.

My hamstrings tingle, but I ignore the sensation. I catch the driver's eyes in the rearview and realize I've seen him before. I smile with purple lips. Purples and blues were the colors we all wore, right down to the shadows and lipsticks. I think we were fairies or something – it doesn't matter much now, I suppose.

Whatever we were supposed to be, I carry the look well. I lick my bottom lip and wink. He looks away. *Too old for him even? Geesh!* Then I notice him looking again, the corner of his eyes lifting slightly.

"Bad audition?" he asks. Before I can answer, he yells "Suck it!" to a driver who swerves in the lane next to us.

"It's all one big learning experience," I say.

"This rain is killing me today, sweetheart. Sorry for my mouth. Yeah, auditions...I bet. I bet there is always something you can do better. I used to feel that way when I played baseball."

"Baseball? The difference, um, what's your name?"

"Max."

"The difference, Max, is that you don't get rejected for being old. Your acceptance is based on performance alone. Me, I'm kicking these kids' asses and still getting the boot."

"I bet you are," he says, with a touch of sleaze that I kind of like.

The next morning, Max looks from me to the disco ball shimmering above his head. He stretches, a faint smile across his face, and asks me to join him at the donut shop – his day job – where he will "hook me up" with a cruller. "We're hiring too, if you're looking for work to, um, supplement your career."

I tell him I have to get started on my YouTube channel. It's still raining outside, and when he gets his pants on and ventures toward the window, I smile, because I know he's going to curse at the sky before he does. I feel connected to him in this strange way.

He yells at the rain, calls it an *inconvenience and an asshole.* Nature is an asshole, I agree, and I look down at my hands. Liver spots –the grossly named logo of old age, of out-of-work acrobats and contortionists. I never looked at my hands when I was younger. My hands were tools; holding me up, twisting my body around, and facilitating my trademark *Ta da!* As audiences used their own hands to clap, my soft young hands did their work.

I watch Max drive off, toss his number on my desk. My computer's camera is not the best, but it will have to do. I dim the lights for mood and tell the camera hello. Then I turn it off and begin to practice. I practice for hours, visualize the flips. I recall my old routine, but add more flourish. I ignore calls, and I continue on. I give it my all. I can. And, I will.

The next day, with the camera pointed my way – taking in my smiling pink lips and black leotard with the reflective strips – I introduce myself once again. I fold backward and feel resistance. My hamstrings ache. But I spring up and back then land on my feet; with only a slight waver, I lift my torso with strength. My chest swells toward the ceiling, and I reach up like a superhero.

The impossible move, the one thing I've never been able to do, was just executed, expertly, in front of the world. It is here, at the top of my game, that I think about Max and how much I'll love to quit all this and join him at that donut shop for chalky coffee. I can even taste the doughy sugar of a fresh cruller melting on my tongue, but the rain doesn't want to stop. The roads are flooding, and here I am watching, waiting for the first thumbs-up.

A HANDBOOK FOR
SINGLE MOTHERS

The girls crash into each other and then the wall. A jumble of screams and giggles pervade the hallway as Cassandra's neighbors, kids themselves, bang something blunt against their side of the wall. Concentrating to steady her hand, she squints, painting her nails a dark purple that is almost black; dark nails signify control over one's domain, the willingness to fight. Red means an all-out battle for dominance, and she doesn't want to go that far.

"Shut! Up!" The neighbors' voices are muffled by thick plaster. *Control today*, Cassandra reminds herself. There is a brief moment of silence before another loud scream and another muffled yell.

"Stop it, girls! It's too early for improv. If the Johns report us again, we'll be in deep shit." The Johns are IT students, one from Nigeria and one from Southern Ohio, and they are especially intolerant of disruptive noise.

Endurance: A Handbook for Single Mothers, page 45, paragraph 2: "Crossed arms (alternately akimbo), wide legs, and a close-mouthed smile create a power posture." Power postures are particularly important when speaking to preteens. Cassandra tests the position as she stands in the doorway. The girls have scarves fastened around their necks with hair clips. Gretchen wears a gold bandana. She jumps on the futon, turns to her mother, and lifts a detached broom handle—her scepter.

"You must understand, Mother, I cannot be stopped now. I have found my power. I seduced and murdered Celina's husband, and now I will rule the kingdom."

"You killed my husband?" Celina gasps.

"I smothered him with my giant breasts. Breasts the size of cantaloupes. I watched him wither." She cups her imaginary cantaloupes.

"It was *you*? *You* murdered my husband? Well then, I will murder you. And I will deflate your cantaloupes with my dagger!" Celina lunges with an imaginary weapon in her hand. "And my army of giant earthworms will devour your soul."

Gretchen falls to the ground, clutching her chest. She's wearing Jacqui's old boots. They come up to her calves. She kicks them in the air, back and forth, before going still.

Cassandra claps, fingers spread, then widens her stance. Sometimes she worries that the girls will never grow up, that she stifled them in some way; other days she worries they're too smart for their own good. "Brava! Chore time. Now!"

"We're on it," Gretchen says.

"We'll get to work, Mom. We're your perfect angels," Celina adds with a curtsy.

If Jacqui were here, she would command them to freeze, and they would, like mannequins, until she decided to free them from her spell. The two straighten their backs and march out of the room.

Cassandra posted a spreadsheet near the fridge that she updates regularly (another trick she picked up from *Endurance*). She assigns the girls various tasks that they are to complete by Monday morning each week. The girls always need help to remember it's there, but once they do, they make a game of it—finding pure enjoyment critiquing each other's work with theatrical efficiency.

"I see a coffee stain left in the bottom of Mom's mug. Mom's mug is precious. Precious mugs are clean mugs."

"That toilet needs to shine. I want to be able to make a peanut butter sandwich on that toilet and eat it without coming down with typhoid. I want to be able to see my reflection in that sink."

"You call this a clean dish?"

"You call this a made bed?"

"We breathe this dust! Look at this! Unacceptable. Do your job, or I'll tell the queen."

"The queen isn't here. The queen is gone forever."

"Mom!"

"Mom!"

Cassandra usually drinks ginger tea to settle her stomach these weekend mornings, hoping there won't be a text from work. Sometimes she cries from sheer exhaustion. Sometimes she feels okay. She always feels the empty space where Jacqui and Greg used to be, if only for a passing moment. Today, she gathers her purse and phone – and ventures out – pleading with the girls to be mindful of the Johns.

The North High Street Library, which connects to Stone Oak Park in North Columbus, was once Cassandra's favorite place. The park seemed brighter when she was a pudgy eight-year-old kid in a pale-pink bathing suit. It also seemed busier, more romantic, and even though the public pool that once cost a quarter is now a vibrant sunken garden, lovely and fragrant, it doesn't feel as glamorous.

Everything is too perfect now, a touched-up photograph. People book the newly built gazebo for marriages and reunions. Festivals are held here in early summer and late autumn. Cassandra remembers holding Jacqui's hand and leading her into the library at least twice a week for story time, how she used to pull ahead, especially on the days when the event coordinator dressed up as a literary character. The days when there was still hope Greg would return, healthy and whole, and Cassandra's family would be complete; he was salvageable then.

Jacqui stands by the tennis courts – walking as though a strong breeze is carrying her along – but the air is still around Cassandra and making her sweat. Her oldest girl, never afraid, never intimidated. Always angry. But maybe this critique isn't entirely fair.

Jacqui's hair is scarlet, an unnatural but flattering shade that sets off her hazel eyes. She's accompanied by a slender man who wears black pants that bunch around his ankles and look tight enough to render him infertile; his extreme side part is emphasized by too much hair gel. The two exhale vapors near an aged *No Smoking* sign.

When she notices Cassandra, Jacqui's eyes roll up and back. Cassandra is an annoyance to her, a small fly buzzing around her head, a stone in her shoe. Jacqui reaches for her partner's hand, and the two swing their arms like a pendulum for a few seconds. He leans on the fence while she saunters toward her mother.

That walk.

Unlike her sisters – who were just toddlers when Cassandra told Greg to never come back after he stumbled into the glass coffee table and fell, shattering her patience and causing yet another mess – Jacqui had understood the arguing, the sickness, and crying from those early days.

The girl was self-sufficient, would have made a respectable Girl Scout, if only Cassandra could have afforded the time to enroll her then; Jacqui was always telling her mother how important preparation was. She asked to learn how to change a tire and wanted to help in the kitchen or make her own dinners. She picked things up quickly, imitating the adults she met and often improving on their efforts. Sometimes she would close her eyes and walk around the townhome – feeling her way up and down the stairs and around the kitchen – retrieving a bottle of juice and then the glass without looking. She would sometimes cheat as she poured.

"What if I lose sight, Mom? I want to be ready."

The day Greg came back the first time, Cassandra felt equal parts fear and relief. Celina and Gretchen had been wary about meeting a father they barely remembered, but to Jacqui, he could do no wrong. He arrived at the front porch with the self-assurance of a stray walking into the place and claiming it as his own.

"Honey, I'm home!" As if he was never gone. He'd been a drunk but also addicted to this and that, and he claimed he was ready to make amends. He looked good, with his dark hair – a little salt around the ears now – cut short and his beard trimmed; he was hardly the mountain man she remembered. "I'm ready now," he said. He said it again. He said it till she believed him.

Cassandra still felt the weight of his deception all those years leading up to the end, his disregard, the mirage. Greg had bags and bags, but nowhere to be. He slept on the couch for the first week, and the girls tiptoed around him.

"He's kind of strange, Mom. Are you sure he's our real dad?"

"I bet he's Gretchen's dad, and not mine."

"Are you kidding? He's as skinny as you. You two look exactly alike. Two straight lines, a sideways equal sign," Gretchen said.

"I'm here to make amends," they both mocked behind his back. And though Cassandra dissuaded this behavior, she secretly relished it because it reminded her to be cautious.

Greg tiptoed around, gracefully, gratefully. Then, late one evening, the two stayed up talking. Before Cassandra knew it, he was unbuttoning her blouse, and she felt ten years younger. "We are one," he whispered, his short beard brushing her earlobe. He poured her a glass of wine. "We are an entity, a partnership."

Cassandra and Greg had wanted to be artists when they met in junior college, and Greg reminded her of those days. They recalled all the movies they always tried to watch and never finished. They tried so many times to watch a movie in its entirety, only to end up entangled on the couch. "Good thing we didn't have the money to go out to movies back then," Greg said.

He slung an arm across her chest the next morning. It was early, a few hours before she planned to wake up for work. "Let's start a business," he said with the same old exuberance. "Think about how successful we could be if we did something out of the box. Pet portraits." She turned to him, and listened. "Think about it! Think about how much people gush over their pets. We'd be specialists. No one else is doing it." Cassandra doubted this was true, but because he seemed to think it'd work, maybe it could. Greg was a new man, and Cassandra convinced herself that she was being romanced all over again. It did seem her blood pumped a little faster when he was around, but it could be pure adrenaline. He got a part-time job at a gas station. He said he'd help more with the bills soon.

Greg never drank, not once, and never showed any hint of going back to his old ways. He volunteered to help out with his daughters as much as possible. He took Jacqui to her friends' homes, to the mall, to school. He even bought a cap that he called his *driver's cap* and would open the back door for his daughter as though she were royalty. She was. That year, that single year in which Cassandra and Greg dated and got to know each other again, the three girls and two parents seemed a perfect family, a collective force, capable of anything.

There were exceptions, of course. After two pet portraits that turned out to be more costly than anything ("Are you kidding me? This isn't Fluffy; there's no white streak on her nose. How could you miss the white streak? It's right there in the photo!"), Greg got a full-time job at the local hardware store and began contributing more financially. He asked Cassandra to make him an honest man.

"Will you?" he asked simply, offering a small solitaire.

Cassandra looked at the ring as though it were a crystal ball, and she saw struggle. She saw herself pawning it five years later when he would disappear again. She saw fights, the girls being caught. She felt the romance, a fire in her shoulders, burn away.

"No," she said. "I'm sorry, but no."

Women should stop apologizing for their feelings or decisions, Cassandra has since read. *Never use the word sorry when you mean a thing.*

"We understand, Mom," Gretchen said.

"We do," Celina agreed.

Jacqui said nothing at all when Cassandra told her that she and Greg had decided it was best he move out. The girl's eyes, soft like her father's, flattened, and she was gone soon after he moved. A note left behind stated she was old enough to make her own decisions, and she was going to live with her father.

The woman walking toward Cassandra today is far from the child who left a few months before. This woman intimidates her. Cassandra feels her hands curling into fists and catches herself, tells herself that her defensive thoughts are just neurons firing, electricity. She assumes her power stance. After all, Jacqui is just a girl, a girl in a woman's body, who will one day understand.

"Cassandra," Jacqui says, sticking her hand out formally.

"Come on, Jacqui. Really?"

"What? You want me to call you *Mom*? Fine, whatever. I'll call you what you want. Mom. How are you, *Mom*?"

Cassandra tells herself to answer without defense. "I'm well. Your sisters are well. A little crazy, but really, really…" Jacqui's face softens at the mention of her sisters. She has been calling from her father's house from time to time, just not to speak to Cassandra. Celina was first to hear that Greg was back to drinking.

"Celina is in theater with Gretch now, and she takes gymnastics at Thompson's. The girl is made of rubber," Cassandra says, noticing Jacqui's rigidness ease. "She bounces and stretches like…like that little toy you used to play with, the green one. The guy with the angular head."

"Gumby, Mom. Yeah. That's good. Gretch?"

"Theater, theater, and more theater. She lives and breathes it now. Good at math. Not sure where she gets that."

"Math makes my eyeballs itch," Jacqui says casually, forgetting her defenses a moment. She catches herself, and her face hardens again. "Why did we have to meet? I haven't changed my mind.

I'm not coming home. I'm almost an adult, so there's really no point."

Cassandra pulls her long blonde-gray braid over one shoulder and takes a moment before speaking again. How should she tackle this? What does *Endurance* say? *Make the other person think it is her idea. Make it seem as though you don't have as much at stake as you do. Be prepared to walk away disappointed. Don't beg!* "Please come home, Jacqui."

"Mom. Black fingernails. Really?"

"You like them? They're not quite black."

"No! Not on you."

"You find them intimidating?"

Jacqui laughs, and her strange friend walks up to join them. "Hey, guys, sorry to interrupt, but there's a bus we gotta catch." He gives her a look.

"We're going to a concert, Mom, and it's a long bus ride."

Had Jacqui read her book? *Structure a time delay, elongate the discussion. If you want power of negotiation, you have to control time.* Jacqui says, "So, Mom, I'm not coming back, but I think you should know that Daddy's in that program again. He's okay, just had a slip or something. He needs me to help out. We can't *all* abandon him."

"No, Jacqui, no, I don't think we should. Come back, and we'll go see him and support him together, but you'll be safe."

"He's not dangerous, Mom."

"But he *is*. When he's drunk, he is." A mistake. The discussion is now an argument, and all the rage in Jacqui's face shows like a map of the future that doesn't include Cassandra.

"Tell my sisters that I'll call them when I can. Goodbye, *Cassandra*."

Weeks devour days, then months. Jacqui rarely reaches out, and when she does, it's indirectly, through Gretchen and Celina, as before. Then, the inevitable day: Cassandra answers the phone and is told that Greg is in trouble.

"He just took off. All we can do is notify the emergency contact. He made it through hard days, a shame really," the nurse says with a sigh. "Also, I think you should know…he was showing signs of liver failure. It is important that he self-correct quickly."

Cassandra knocks on Greg's apartment door, which is red and in line with a series of other red apartment doors that look just like it. The red doors disturb her.

He lives in a balcony apartment that overlooks a basketball court with deep cracks in the asphalt. Cassandra imagines Jacqui coming home here after school, sleeping on the couch, and getting propositioned by the young men in the neighborhood as she walks to the bus stop.

Cassandra calls so many times that the hollow sound of ringing echoes when she tries to sleep.

"Girls, talk to your sister if she calls. Tell her she needs to come home," Cassandra says.

"We'll do what we can," they both say.

"Listen, girls, I need you to take this seriously. Be soldiers." The two girls, all preteen determination and awkward physicality—one thin and one plump—stand straight and nod.

"Operation Jacqui Home," Gretchen says.

"We need to work the angle of the odd boy," Celina says.

"Are they dating?" Cassandra asks.

"They're not dating. He's gay," Gretchen says.

"He's androgynous," Celina says. "His name is Michael, or Michele or something."

"Let's focus on the target herself, girls," Cassandra says. "What are her soft spots?"

"Daddy. Saving people. Coffee with too much sugar. Boys. Being told she's pretty."

"She said she's painting now, Mom. She said she wants to move to New York City."

Cassandra wishes she knew more about her daughter's life. Together they decide that when Jacqui reaches out, they'll appeal to her sense of empathy. They'll say there's an emergency, so she feels compelled to help. It isn't the most honorable plan, but it is for the greater good.

The first time Jacqui calls to say hi, however, Gretchen gets nervous and starts talking too fast. Summoning all her theatrics, she says, "We were trying to get ahold of you. Come home. Now. Celina's—her foot is mangled—freak accident. It's all infected now. We're worried." She fumbles the phone and hangs up. "Mom? Mom? I kind of messed up the plan."

The smoke and fresh air feel necessary, a little too necessary. Cassandra keeps an emergency cigarette for times like this. Both Johns smoke, but it surprises her nonetheless when they both emerge wearing jeans and rivaling sports jerseys. They are vaping, the thing kids do, and Cassandra thinks she'll try it. "Cool day," John in the white jersey says.

"You guys nearing finals?" Cassandra asks absently.

"Not till May," John in the blue jersey says. "I didn't know you smoke."

"I don't. My daughter's coming over. The oldest."

"The mean one?"

"The oldest. The youngest told her a lie to get her over here. She's going to flip."

"You're nothing like my mom," Blue Jersey says. He examines her a moment, as though deciding whether to elaborate. "If I ran away like that, even to stay with any of my hillbilly relatives, she would have found me, grabbed me by the ear, and made my ass come back home."

"Your kids run you, yeah?" White Jersey says.

"What?" Were they really saying this, she wonders. She wants to retaliate, but the smoke hits her stomach the wrong way. She takes the power stance.

"Strong personalities, those girls. That's got to come from somewhere. But, no, they do not run me."

Cassandra looks down at her red polish, another power color, which is chipping at the corner of each thumb. She takes a long drag on her cigarette, stale and rough on her throat, ignoring her desire to throw up, and examines the Johns.

They're just kids, but they're right. Cassandra needs to take charge. She needs more than dark polish.

Just as she's about to ask them what she should do, exactly, what their moms would do, Jacqui appears at the end of the street. In all black, she walks toward them as quickly as possible in chunky heels with her hair piled on her head like a nest. Cassandra can see the overdone makeup from half a block away.

"You know what, guys? Thanks. Thank you. If there's noise in the next hour, deal with it." She puts out the cigarette and walks toward her daughter, meeting her at the step.

"Mom." Jacqui starts running toward Cassandra. "Is she okay? Is she at the hospital? What the hell happened? Gretchen said that little C was in an accident, that something crushed her foot and hand. They're not broken, are they? Why aren't we at the hospital? Was it one of those John idiots? Were you waiting for me? Is Gretchen there? How does that happen?"

Cassandra simply nods back and forth, slowly. "There was no accident."

"Really? Really, Mom?" Jacqui doesn't breathe; her words are dry and fierce. "I'm going to kill them." She rushes for the door, but Cassandra's slender hands grab her daughter's shoulders, squeezing and pulling back. "Ouch!"

The two Johns go inside, but open their blinds.

"Let's walk, child."

"Child? What the hell, Mom?" Cassandra notices she said *Mom*. She gestures toward the sidewalk, which leads to a small park.

"I want you to come home, but your sisters want it as well. They didn't go about it in the right way, I admit, but they were just trying to get your attention. They miss your face. They miss your brooding and your dry humor and your attitude. Jacqui, they need you."

"Dad needs me, too. Why don't you understand that? He needs me more. No one gives two shits about him. You didn't want him, and he fell apart. He's sick, Mom. He needs me. He tells me he needs me." Cassandra still has her by the arm, blood-colored nails digging into her pale skin.

"You need to explain that to your sisters." She pulls Jacqui, expecting her to break away and go running down the street. Instead, the girl wilts, offers a pleading look.

"He needs us, Mom. I'm not the one running away here."

Cirrhosis is the villain that has trapped Greg in the hospital. The girls call it his dungeon. Only a few people from AA visit. His parents died in a car accident some years before, and he has alienated most of his friends. Cassandra trades weak smiles with those few visitors. They are kind and supportive. A woman in a red sweater offers Cassandra her phone number and says to call anytime, day or night. "He always talked about you, you know. I'm good at helping people. And you don't gotta be an addict to need a sponsor."

Cassandra takes the girls to see him on weekends, four weekends exactly, before his slender body deflates. Cassandra stays up nights and sits by the window. Jacqui feeds him spoonfuls of applesauce long after her sisters stop joking and begin to stare out the window or doze off while watching TV. Michele sometimes visits, too, and he's a nice kid, if painfully shy. He lets Gretchen and Celina braid his long hair and beat him in card games. He teaches Cassandra how to play chess, and she wins – or he lets her win – after a few games.

The girls take turns breaking down, sobbing and excusing themselves into the hall and curling up in the back seat of the car when they drive home. Jacqui walks him to the bathroom – the good days, when he can get up. She wipes bits of regurgitated applesauce off his chin. She salvages a few of his paintings from his apartment before the eviction and hangs them in the hospital room.

"She is the queen, our sister. Our sister the queen," Celina and Gretchen say, trying to make her laugh the day she returns with her bags. They pile all the pillows in her room on top of one another and hoist their sister, an eighteen-year-old woman, beautiful and slight, to the top. "The queen has returned."

The day the call comes, it is an hour before they are headed to the hospital. Cassandra searches for the little square of paper from the woman in the red sweater before she tells her daughters. The woman graciously absorbs her tears so that the girls won't have to.

Greg would be cremated. Cassandra and the girls would drive his ashes to Virginia Beach, a stretch he once told Cassandra he'd been to as a kid. "It was the only family trip we'd ever been on that didn't end in a war," he'd said. "It was magic."

The four of them sit on the beach, their bodies sinking into wet sand. Jacqui's head is heavy on Cassandra's shoulder. The girls are silently building shapes of unnamed things. Waiting.

The waves and wind move together as the girls spread their father's ashes. He is the ocean now. Jacqui – for the first time since her father left her so many years ago – needs her mother, so Cassandra holds her. She holds them all. The water kisses their feet.

.

A PERPETUAL STATE OF AWE

We count to three and pull hard to gain an inch of light. The ice around the door gives, and a clump of snow is released. The fresh air feels nice for a moment before it begins to bite at our cheeks. Yesterday's snow is now an undercoat, and the powdery top layer glistens.

"Looks like it's winking at the sky," Joshua says.

There is nothing but snow, expectant clouds, and the top halves of our neighbors' homes. A few still have smoke escaping from their chimneys.

"Nature's secret," I say, trying to match his detached tone. The wonderland covers cars and bikes; it climbs stairs and devours porches. Our doors are barricaded with only a few feet uncovered at the top.

Joshua backs up and sighs as he grabs the broom. I lean all my weight in, hoping the door will close easily today, but it doesn't budge. He sweeps at our warped wood floors.

"We're lucky to be on the north side of Grant Avenue, kiddo," I say. Joshua hates it when I call him *kiddo*, but he lets me off the hook. He examines the slight incline toward the other side of the street. We were spared at least a foot of accumulation. He lingers in the doorway, and a thin arm of sunlight reaches in and warms my face; meanwhile, the icy air and brilliant light begin to crowd around us. We push the door again, together, but it still resists.

We had been enjoying the snow a few days ago. Joshua suggested it would be our new way of life – sleds instead of cars –and that it was nature's way of eliminating overuse of fossil fuels. The whole town seemed thrilled to be off from work and school. Kids slid down the street on cardboard boxes, and we all started fires and roasted marshmallows together, contributing thermoses of hot chocolate and warm sandwiches, finding communal warmth.

We watched the news for the latest soup recipes. Potato and leek was featured the same day the grocery stores closed for good. Joshua and I were playing Scrabble by the fire when the lights began to flicker. Neighbors stopped venturing outside. There were talks of delaying holidays, and online retailers pleaded their customers' forgiveness as shipping would no longer be possible.

Another night of snow, and the wrinkles deepened around newscasters' eyes, gazes tilted downward; they forced hollow smiles. The mail stopped altogether. Reception faded in and out more frequently, and it comprised reports of missing persons and bodies found frozen in their homes. There had been just under a thousand fatalities from Cleveland to Columbus, and we received texts with the lists of names. There was no news from outside of Ohio, so we were left to imagine how much worse things must be up north.

The snow started coming down with more force, almost violence, and on the tenth day of accumulation, we heard what sounded like a stampede, only to look out the window and see Mr. Henry's roof caving in under the weight and cold. We lost power completely. More roofs crumbled and generators gave out; my cell became my final digital connection, but I couldn't recharge it, so I kept it off.

I have an ounce of power left now, if that, and am scared to turn the phone on and lose everything. My son is calm, so I have to pretend to be calm along with him. The kid's calm doesn't surprise me, even though he's a nervous wreck at school, and agonizes over what to wear and what to say and whether he'll do well in spelling or chess championships. I've had to physically drag him to the car the first few days of school each year.

Shortly before the storm, one of Joshua's teachers called, worried that Joshua never spoke to kids his age and spent his recesses asking teachers what they thought of technology convergence and its potential to break down capitalism as we know it. "He's smart," she explained, "but he doesn't know how to relax."

John and I agreed to begin family sessions. In therapy, we could come clean. We were still leading our son – and maybe each other – to believe that we could work things out. Deep down, however, we knew there was no chance.

"We'd better find someone brilliant, or else Josh'll run mental circles around him. He gets that from you, you know," John said the last time we spoke.

"I don't think he gets it from either of us."

John chuckled, and I asked him when he'd be stopping by. He said soon.

I doubt that Joshua fully believed us about much of anything. He had always challenged our assertions when he was younger until the day he stopped. The day, I assume, he realized there was no point. After he turned eleven or so, I couldn't keep up with the kid's mind, and I surely can't now that he's fifteen. But I didn't need him to show me how he could memorize a deck of cards to know he was special; Joshua has always kept me in a perpetual state of awe.

"Time," he says.

"No way."

"Just two minutes, Mom. We can't go all the way outside, but we can open the window." Joshua insists on going out incrementally longer every day to adjust to the cold and increase odds of survival. He wants me to do the same, but I can't. Nor can I stop him. "Come on, Mom. Two minutes. One. This is going to be life or death if they don't arrive soon."

"I can't," I say.

He speaks urgently now, can tell something is wrong with me. "We can tunnel, melt, and pack the snow. I've been thinking, and – " He goes on, problem solving, but I'm dizzy and unable to concentrate.

It'd taken damn near all my strength getting the door open a crack, and I can't fathom the idea of standing outside. The cold is the enemy. I've been eating less as our food dwindles, pretending to be full, so the boy can eat more, and it's catching up to me.

"We have to dig," he says again.

"Let me just sit here and think a minute, okay?" I say, easing onto the couch and putting my hood back up over my ears. I sound vaguely drunk.

I haven't seen a car drive anywhere in two weeks, and the last person to walk by our home was Mr. Henry, and I haven't seen his lights go on since his roof fell. One of his windows had shattered. The cold is too much for anyone, let alone someone his age.

My cell gives me what I'm sure is its final warning when I power it on, so I write down everything from the Storm Emergency Instructions text we all got before losing power. It contains hints and tips, assurances that FEMA is on the way, and the last list of names – those missing as of Friday – cataloged by zip code.

"A new way of life," I repeat, scooting to a part of the couch that was touched by the sun. "I think this ice is too thick to melt. I think we'll have to wait for someone to come."

More snow pushes its way in, dusts Joshua's boots. "Look," he says, pointing. From the crack, we watch as the snow a few feet away shakes slightly. I think I might be imagining it until he says, "Something is moving beneath the surface." I examine the instructions I copied again and feel a twinge of hope.

A muffled sound, a man's voice, says, "We are," then goes quiet.

"See, someone's out there. Maybe we can help." Joshua gathers all our cleaning fluids and pours some electric blue cleaner into a large squirt bottle. He sprays at the base of the door, then nudges snow to the left with his boot. I stare at my phone and scroll down to John's name while my son is still busy.

Joshua can't know – won't know, not now. He thinks his father is safe, or at least out of town on business as usual. It was an easy lie, and it was in place before the snowfall. Our separation wasn't official yet, after all, and I believed him when he said he was coming soon. When I couldn't get ahold of him last week, I knew.

I stare at his name, illuminated, then blurry. My phone flickers off and something inside of me goes with it. I stand up, only to sit right back down, dizzy.

The muffled voice arrives again, and this time we hear the entire message. "We are here to help. We are tunneling to each residence. Please bundle up," he says. "Please continue to chip away where you can. Again, if you can hear this message, we are tunneling toward you. Please stay warm. Please stay calm. Remove any snow that you can."

Chances of survival drop quickly after an avalanche, and suffocation or asphyxia sets in after approximately thirty to forty minutes, depending on the weight of the snow and the air available. I did not copy this bit down, but it repeats in my mind, a forced mantra. Joshua stops and starts, stops and starts. He is spraying as quickly as he can. Then the blue liquid is gone, and there is a dent in the snow the size of a baseball.

"Take a break, kiddo. I've got this for a while." I look at his hands after he takes off his gloves. They are a deep purple, almost as bad as mine, and his face has gone solid, as though it's frozen. "You okay, baby?"

"I'm shaking," he says. I reach out my arm.

"This isn't magic at all," I say.

FEMA does not arrive that night, but I hear more announcements and stay up, unable to close my eyes. I am rocking my son as though he is young again. Crashing sounds reverberate, and I feel like I'm in a cosmic waiting room. Just a month ago, I was agonizing over which heels to wear with my new suit, a suit I believed would land me a new position. Now I am swathed in thick cloth – a cacophony of clothes and blankets – and I am barely able to stand.

I know it's coming before it does. As Joshua sleeps, the ceiling begins to crack. The crack is a slow-moving animal, opening its mouth slightly. I look toward the kitchen and see that the ceiling there is worse. The lights are gone. There is no basement to run to, no outside, no nothing. I hold my son, listen to the creaks of shifting beams and the soft explosions above us.

"Honey," I say, waking him. I don't know why I wake him, except maybe to give him a little more time. Even fear is life. Pure life. He looks up and his face has reddened at the cheeks. The sound of glass breaking outside our door tears at my stomach.

"I want to make my son soup," I say.

"Mom?"

"I want to give him more life," I say.

"Mom, I'm right here. They can't hear you yet."

133

A sharp object splinters the wood of our door, and as I feel the cold again, I realize I am dozing off. "Sorry, kiddo. Sorry."

A bundle of fur and cloth breaks down our door, and I can see two eyes, brown and reddened at the rims, and I think of the cucumber martini with the chili rim I drank with John the night we decided to split. I feel an icy arm lift me up.

"Your mother is in shock," a man says. "We'll carry her. We have a safe place to take you. We have food." He places something warm in my hands.

I close my eyes and, just like that, I am resting my head on John's shoulder, warm, listening to my son practice his definitions. My thoughts all cluster together, a cold mass. I feel myself move a little. I run my thumb across my fingertips. The man has taken my son outside and is helping me toward the door, when I hear another loud crack and then see crumbling at the ceiling.

"I'm fine now," I say. And as the man nods and leads me out, I continue to look up. I see him reach for me, but this is not his choice.

I feel pieces of my home fall, ricochet off my back. We head into the narrow tunnel, and when I look back, there is darkness. There is nothing. The house and snow are caving in around us. I try to push forward, but nature has already decided. Joshua has grabbed my arm. "Your father," I say, but he stops me, says he knows and it's okay. His blood is thick now; he will survive.

"It's a new way of life," I say.

After a dark blanket is thrown over my eyes, I begin to feel warmer. John is still holding me. My son forgives us. We are all safe. There are two bodies, fur and cloth, reaching for me in the background – strong bodies, thick blood – but they begin to flicker out. I tell them I don't want to leave now. I am home. I embrace my family gently as the snow caves in. The snow is generous, framing us in an eternal portrait. It doesn't take forty-five minutes. It doesn't even take thirty. It takes no time at all.

NEBRASKA

The grocery aisles are crammed with bodies. The owners of J&J's are stopping people at the door. The fire department never gave an exact occupancy limit because there was never a need, until recently, but it only takes a bit of common sense to tell this is a fire hazard. I give up on the cereal aisle, don't even consider the produce, and reevaluate my need for peanut butter.

I can see the local brand, Mary Ellen's, on the bottom shelf. I imagine spreading it thick on a grainy piece of toast. It won't be around forever, this brand. Mary Ellen's daughter recently sold the company to Walzon Corporation, and it will soon be like all the others – Wally's (additive soup). I will miss this peanut butter. I will miss it with honey and miss it with jam. Since I moved to Marquette, I've perfected my own recipe for an apple-pear butter that I sell at the farmer's markets on Saturdays, and boy does Mary Ellen's all-natural, extra-smooth peanut butter complement my fruit butter.

I wait, widening my stance so as not to be pushed over, as the masses shove and shift, and I slowly make my way closer to the jar with the brown top and yellow bow. A woman wearing a summer dress and silver sandals moves her cart out of the way as she gossips to someone on her cell. She recounts some story about some pop star on some show who has an extra nipple and apparently breastfeeds with it, which the woman, I gather, finds tasteless and unnatural. I think about my childhood, long before folks in Los Angeles and Phoenix, Chicago, and Tallahassee started growing skin tags that morphed into whole new body parts.

It didn't take long for it to happen in all major cities. Some were born with extra parts whereas others were born missing things – eyelashes or fingernails, a bottom lip that demanded eating machinery or a tendon that required a synthetic and caused a person to favor one side. It affected the rich first. Plastic surgery was phased out, then unnecessary pills, then all plastic water bottles. After none of these measures did much, people decided it was the food and began to move toward the center of the states – a fast-moving migration to the Midwest that has caused me one hell of a headache.

I stare at the two rows of toes on each of her feet before she is swallowed by the crowd. There are four people between me and the peanut butter, so I keep my eyes tight on the jar as I wait for an opening I can slip through to get to it. This little store used to have one to five customers max, especially on a Monday afternoon.

Everyone wants a share of the farm life because things are clean here, relatively. The allergens are natural. The dirt is not radioactive – and often even fertile – and the rain is still the color of water. There are folks in the big cities yet; folks in Houston are hanging on, as are those in Seattle, but it will only be a matter of time. The papers say so. There are community holes broadening in each state, and the middle-class are following the rich.

I moved here when I was younger, before all the hype and glamour attached to Nebraska. It was either Marquette or Benton, and when I visited Marquette I knew it was right. I suppose I was an early adopter. "A simpler way of life" was how it was being sold then – farm life was a brand-new advertising initiative on the Internet then, and small-town governments were cleaning house as one downtown after another began to show signs of self-destruction. Back then, there were fellowships and meditation retreats in which people walked mindfully through corn. It all looked so exotic and peaceful. I never thought I'd look back after moving here from Cleveland, but this is ridiculous. I move forward and can almost reach the jar. I try and come a foot or so short.

I have to mix this particular brand of peanut butter two or three minutes. I don't mind because it is some seriously wonderful peanut butter. The only man blocking me now is wearing overalls, which I appreciate, and his hands are dirt-stained. He looks vaguely familiar, probably just keeps to himself, but I think I've seen him at the farmer's market. He's reading the label of a jar of "Wally's" Walzon peanut butter with a critical eye.

"Excuse me," I yell, and a kid runs between us, almost knocking my shopping cart over. "That kind isn't so good. I tried it a while back. It's all artificial." I point to my brand, and he stares at me a long time. His eyes are flat, blue, but I think I can see some amusement in them. He thinks I'm a joke, another one of the hundreds in this grocery on their smartphones, missing the entire point of moving here. When I moved here, the town was 248 people, and this grocery accommodated them easily. Now there are 1,042, and only this one grocery, until the Walzon Plus is built down the road. Aside from the farmer's market, there's nowhere else to buy much of anything save the dollar store, so J&J's is going to be like this awhile.

Overalls doesn't say anything, but he grabs a jar of my recommended brand, and when he does I realize it was the only one. I could get crunchy then try to put it in my food processor. I suppose I could make my own peanut butter, all truth told, but something in me ignores the buy-local-sell-local mantra in my head, and I pick up a jar of the processed stuff as someone behind me mumbles, "Hurry up."

I am pushed and shoved and elbowed, so I push and shove and elbow. The construction outside is head-splitting. Houses are being built everywhere, exact replicas of each other excepting the color of the paint, or the direction the garage is facing. Everyone who came from money owns the expensive equipment; the green and yellow of the freshly cleaned and waxed backhoes glisten in the sun. I tend to just mosey around on an old ATV and read meters and make my jams and pies for the farmer's market, and I really loved this life till recently. I am almost to the checkout when I realize I'm missing sugar.

I say excuse me no less than a dozen times, but all the folks headed toward me create an impenetrable wall. I call out, then see the orange flag of a clerk and ask if she can get me some sugar; she just rolls her eyes and waves her flag the direction of the registers, so I leave my cart and rush – best I can – toward the baking aisle. Weaving in and out of bodies connected to electrical devices – so many dazed that they don't notice me crawling between their legs or nudging them with my country-wide butt and hips to get by – I grab the biggest bag I can carry so that I won't have to return to this horrid place for a few weeks. But when I return to the register line, I can't find my cart. I just wasted an hour, and I feel restless in a way I haven't since I lived in Cleveland. I throw the sugar on the floor, and the bag tears open. A mound of crystal white slowly forms, and everyone around watches it and me like we are the most unrefined combination of anything they've ever seen.

Overalls is sitting on a bench with my favorite peanut butter. He has his foot propped up on the other side, so I edge my way over to him as folks begin to move around again, trampling the sugar and allowing it to coat their boots and high heels. He moves and gestures for me to sit. This empty space is a rarity, and I take a seat, offering him some gum.

"How did this happen?" I ask him. "When I moved here, everything was so quiet. Everyone lived for the land and listened to the land and lived for the – "

"Land, yeah. But people are nature too," he says.

"Yeah okay," I say. "Thanks for that."

He smiles at me, sun wrinkles deepening around his eyes, and he hands me Mary Ellen's natural, extra-smooth peanut butter. I hesitate, but I accept it and tuck it away in my canvas bag. "There are people moving back, you know," he says.

"I don't blame them. I'd do anything to escape these crowds."

"People are nature too," he says again. I shrug, but he nods confidently to reinforce and adds, "When you go, I'll miss your pies."

After sitting a while with Overalls – taking in that special kind of silence only possible in the midst of chaos – I nod my thanks and nudge my way back to the sugar aisle. I even brave the produce, determined to make enough rhubarb and strawberry to tide folks over a while as I head back toward the unknown malformations that await me.

GREEN

An aspiring minimalist, Joseph combated excess with routine. He paid his quarterly waste bills on time and in Bitcoin, overpaying when he anticipated lower commissions. He didn't engage in unnecessary human-to-human interaction, but he Tweeted and posted and shared a minimum of fifty times daily to maintain the fan base for his streaming channel and, in particular, for his leading Thursday night show, *The Many Lives of Art*. He sent private messages to fans and associates on a semi-regular basis in order to foster deeper *friend*ships.

Before he met Alyssa, Joseph had been a Level Three Green Citizen for eighteen months running; his individual footprint was 0.013%, which was notable, as most had a 0.02% average (government worker information not disclosed). He worked hard to maintain this average and was proud of it, but not too proud.

Joseph was alone most of the time. Even though he sometimes missed the regular video chats and occasional physical meetings with Trish, his ex-wife, he was content that he'd had his experience as a husband. Once was enough. One of anything was enough.

Joseph's Achilles' heel was personal transportation. He, somewhat shamefully, owned two bicycles; his mother gave him a hard time about it, and rightfully so. He paid additional taxes for the superfluous bike, and he sometimes thought of selling or donating it. Everyone had at least one indulgence, he reasoned. He used one bike for transport and another for leisure. He preferred it this way because one was always clean and in good shape. There was no better way to come up with ideas for the show than on his leisure bike, among the dwindling natural things.

Joseph's behavior on the road was stellar; he'd considered becoming a cycle cop before settling for a writing career, like 89% of the population (not including government workers). Writing was the safer career path, after all, as there was talk of one day eliminating the need for human transport and mobilizing society by drones alone.

Joseph tended to stay in the second lane to the left, never racing or getting tickets, always respecting the speed limits. He voted every year, not only to keep the roads but to extend them. Biking was visceral, freeing.

Alyssa was digging in Joseph's trash square the Sunday morning they met. He'd wanted to squeeze in a short ride because he was scheduled to have a video conference with his family later that day—most of them lived in Holland, so they had monthly, sometimes bimonthly, visits—and even a quick ride on the leisure bike would help him to mentally prepare himself. He paused in the doorway, rubbed his face a few times to make sure he was awake, and asked, "What the fresh hell?"

Alyssa didn't answer at first. She wore tight jeans and a long, flowing shirt that looked worn but a little too nice for trash digging. Joseph would dig around in his own trash when money was tight or ratings were low, looking for materials to bury or redistribute; but to see someone in his personal trash square made him feel oddly exposed.

She was hinged over at the waist, really digging in with her feet lifted from the ground, so she had to ease herself down. She did this expertly, smiling, holding Joseph's old blender in her hand. She said, "I dropped something in here by accident. Sorry if I woke you. I'll pay a dollar or two – whatever the increase." Her eyes were bright. She seemed to be examining his face to determine whether or not he was convinced, then added, "You can send me your itemized bill. It was just a notebook, a few old poems. Printed copies."

He eyed the blender. "They're talking about making print illegal, you know."

"I know. I just – I like holding them, seeing them off the screen." She glanced beyond him, at the two bikes securely hung on the wall just beyond his front door, and he thought he caught something like intrigue on her face before she put on a phony smile.

He closed the door behind him. "You want me to help? Trash compacts on Mondays here, and I haven't thrown much away, so it has to be near the surface. I haven't taken a shower yet," he said, noticing that her shirt was quite sheer.

"How sweet! No. But can I have this?" she asked, holding up the blender.

"That costs far more than a few papers." Plastic was heavy; she was probably saving Joseph $20 in weight fees. The government weighers for block 7D were merciless with Joseph; he'd pissed them off once by leaving out a broken office chair on the wrong day.

"I'm Alyssa," she said, curtsying. "I'm from Ohio."

"Welcome to block 7D."

The next time Joseph saw Alyssa, she was outside in a light rain, wearing a neon-green ball cap, her short blonde hair tucked behind her ears. She was moving, nimble, flipping and twisting a giant arrow leading the way to the scrap sale on block 7N. Joseph was surprised to see she had a physical job – a rarity – or was she being projected?

He pulled his bike up to the curb, trying to determine whether he was seeing a hologram or a person, and another cyclist honked, annoyed, almost clipping his heels. Joseph hoisted the bike up onto the curb and took a breath, realizing that Alyssa was actually here. *How odd*, he thought.

"Neighbor!"

"I can't believe you do this in real time, in physical form. How long did it take you to get it down? I mean – you have it down. Most of these folks struggle or turn it slowly, and they're at home, recorded. I can't believe you do this live!"

"Thanks. We still have a choice, and I like the rain. I also like to do as much physical stuff as possible for my reality show." She pointed up at the streetlight where a red dot winked at them. "I know it's a lot to ask, but since you stopped. I mean, if you have the time, can you go to the sale?" She pointed to the big arrow. "I get my bonus based on the number of people who walk in the door, so even if you just walk in and walk out – I mean, if you want. I'll watch your bike."

"Why don't I ever see you?" Joseph asked. Granted, he never saw most of his neighbors, but her condo was always dark, and he never heard so much as a rustle outside.

"I like to be out, have my cameras set up everywhere. I get lonely at home."

"You can visit anytime," he offered. "Except right now. I have a scrap sale to go check out." He smiled, felt the distraction welling up in his belly, and didn't bother to shake it off.

She clapped her hand against the arrow and smiled, then turned back to the traffic and began to spin. A man on a pink bike yelled out, asking that she flash him, and Joseph flicked him off.

As soon as he entered the scrap store, vendors began yelling from all directions. They were selling vintage items: pagers, phones, laptops, and even a few Apple products. Joseph smiled to himself, thinking of Alyssa's admission. She was lonely, and this pleased him for some reason.

Before heading out, Joseph paused near a box filled with a couple hundred SIM cards. He liked collecting these for character studies. After finding three or four that had legible ID numbers, he pressed his finger to the payment pad and hurried out. People in the twenty-first century had been so awkward with technology, eager to use every application that existed, wasteful; they'd left sprawling and exposed lives, and Joseph had found this an ideal way to come up with storylines for his show – a drama about a group of struggling artists who try their hands at everything unrelated to art to find their ideas. The cast shifted every season so viewers wouldn't get bored.

When he returned, Alyssa was gone, and his leisure bike – his favorite – was gone with her. He figured she had ridden off as part of her show; perhaps it was a comedy angle or a prank show, which was annoying but understandable seeing as how competition for ratings was fierce. He began to walk home. The walking lanes were nice, and it was a thing he hadn't done in a long time. He had about four miles to go, so he thought about his next story as he took slow steps in the rain.

By the time Joseph got home, his story was basically mind-mapped. His lead artist this season, a character named Eko, would become a professional sign flipper for the show; instead of scrap shops, he would point the way to an old-fashioned circus or animal show. The audience for this season might shift, and Joseph may get some mean comments, but heated discussion boards would only increase his viewership. Animals were no longer forced into captivity, but there was a movement, and many who secretly kept pets from sheer loneliness. They were undisciplined and greedy as far as Joseph was concerned, but he understood.

As soon as he got home, he began to write. He wrote for almost three hours and immediately sent his idea to his agent. She replied with a smiley ping because he was, for once, a week ahead of his deadline.

Stretching his legs, which were oddly sore from the long walk, Joseph choked down his 2 p.m. smoothie, a gray and tasteless thing, then went to knock on Alyssa's door. When she answered, she was naked, but for the sheer flowy shirt he'd seen her wearing the day he met her; her body was as perfect as a human's can get. He asked her if she was still lonely, and she said yes.

Live sex was exhausting to Joseph. After, he listened to her light snoring and enjoyed the wave of distraction. At one time, Trish and Joseph had been an entity; she had been a co-writer on the show; they had shared the bills and the profiles and the bikes; they spoke to family together; they slept together, either online or in person, and she would sometimes snore.

Joseph rolled out of bed slowly, quietly, figuring he'd return later to ask about his bike. She woke up and licked her lips. "I took your bike because you have two. I don't have any. I figured it would be okay," she said sleepily.

Joseph leaned into her, hoping she'd embrace him again, invite him back to bed. Instead, she said, "I can compensate you now. Feel free to check my computer area, and if you prefer, I will return the bicycle." Computer areas were private rooms in most homes, locked up like vaults.

"Do I need a key?"

"No. I'm heading out, though, so just be sure the door closes all the way when you leave."

Joseph nodded. He wondered what she had in mind for payment. Her computer room was lined with purple lights, celebratory. Her avatar greeted him from a screen and asked his name and

Citizen ID number. He told her he wasn't logging in. "Oh yes, the neighbor," the avatar said. "Alyssa has your bike. She would like to know if she can keep it."

"I don't know," he said. "It is extraneous, but I'm attached."

"It is best she keep it, then, don't you think? It's only a matter of time before it is found out."

Joseph took an audible, exasperated breath. He rubbed the back of his neck. "I still want it back. I pay taxes on it."

"I must be honest. The bicycle will not be returned, Joseph. Alyssa is a drifter. Would you like footage from your sexual experiences over the course of the last two days? It's 7K, 4D, with over 40 filters to choose from. You can change hair color and even body shape if you get bored."

He watched as teaser clips were displayed on the wall, and wished he had footage of Trish instead. Despite his desire to fight, he knew the avatar was right. He would have to move on. "Yes, please," he said. "Thank you."

"Anytime. Please give me your hand." A few numbers flashed, and Joseph was asked to remit payment.

"For the digital copy or the sex?" he asked.

"Alyssa takes donations. It is up to you."

"Donations for sex?"

"Donations for her life. Her life is crowdfunded. She will not see you again, I am sure. She liked you, however. She wrote that in a poem."

"We could have meal shakes together," he said. "Maybe I can convince her to return the bike."

"Thank you for the offer, but no. She's busy," the avatar said. "We both are. Alyssa is no longer lonely. She thanks you for coming over to retrieve your bike."

"I would have come over anyway," Joseph assured her avatar. "I still will."

"That would be excessive."

Joseph watched Alyssa again in the footage, Zooming in and changing the angle so that he didn't see himself but gained his perspective again. The quality was truly great. But he had learned his lesson, knew there was no point overdoing anything.

He turned it off and got down to business, deducting the bike from his personal inventory and reaching an all-time low-impact footprint of 0.011%. This was something to tell the family about; they'd be very proud.

Advertisers were relentless. Image after image of new bicycles popped up on his screens. Before taking one of many long walks, he searched Alyssa's name and location, and pulled her up on one of the city's live cameras; she was pedaling in sandals and loose clothes, waving at cameras as she swerved illegally in and out of lanes.

The dark blue paint of the bike shone in the sun as she parked sloppily in someone's bike drive. Joseph watched, mortified, as she let the bike rest under an acorn tree. She hoisted herself up and into someone's trash box, and he shut down the computer, imagining how efficient he would be after the pesky feelings of loss and loneliness passed.

WEST ON N ROAD

Rattle walked the loop at sunrise and sunset. At dawn, he was quick-footed, ignoring joints that ached and scraped as though rusted. He pushed on, to the first big rock, shaking the bones and waking the tendons. The stiffness would ease after a quarter-mile.

Dusk was easier, a stroll. By this time, the joggers, middle-aged scale watchers, and families with hyperactive children shared the path. In the summer, Rattle wore only his blue shorts. He was covered in tattoos, which had bled green from too many suns. Symbols for rebirth and movement, once penned on taut skin, were now shapes with rough outlines that revealed loose, flabby skin. He lived for and inside each symbol. Living inside of them gave him permission to ignore the rest of the world. Rattle's stomach, still muscular behind the drooping, was covered in thick-lined inks for each of the places he lived. From the base of his back grew a leafless tree from which a tiny bird was flying. A snake coiled.

He was alone much of the time, living in a mobile by Blackfoot Lake – a space he rented for $300 a month with no contract. He worked odd jobs, painting and housework, some light construction here and there. He helped install a septic system to hold over his landlords when he was two months late on the rent; every now and again, he was asked to show up to clubs in Lincoln, where he would drink or walk around and talk up strangers who would ask him about his tattoos.

This was a small town, 456 people last census, and it didn't take much to be different.

"Why'd you get so many tattoos?" a boy asked at the last event, his eyes wide but his small hands curled in. He was a tough kid, Rattle could tell, just as he had been.

"I like to remember what happens," Rattle told him.

He was accustomed to people staring or sneaking shots with their cellphones at the park. Children would point. In a way, he enjoyed their reactions. The people who pretended not to notice were the most provoked by his appearance. They were the simple ones. If they looked especially avoidant, he'd bark or howl at them, summoning his inner wolf.

Having completed this loop around the same time every day for almost two months, there were fewer people to unsettle. The regulars waved, said hello. "Hey," he'd say back, or he'd just nod. A runner with a soft build, probably mid-thirties, jogged directly toward him around dawn on a Saturday. She wore a lime-green and pale-purple get-up, cringeworthy and bright. There was no reason to wear such loud things here if you asked Rattle. People didn't need to further distinguish themselves from nature.

The woman stared at him, but not in the usual way. She was straining for breath and wanted to stop to walk, he could tell, but she was pushing through for some reason. Maybe she was afraid. She wasn't fit enough to be training, excepting a first race. It was when she was about to pass him that she picked up her knees and began to sprint.

She stared directly into his eyes, a thing no one did – no matter how unimpressed – until she was behind him. He looked back and noticed that she, too, was looking back. She caught his eyes again in a predatory fashion. Rattle pulled on his long, white beard. The soft woman wanted something from him, but what? Since he had nothing to give, he decided to turn around and continue the loop in the opposite direction.

Cirrus clouds were breaking apart like stretched cotton, making way for fatter, darker clouds. The sky before a storm had set the stage for so many decisions in Rattle's life. But rain today was not the pleasure it once was. Rain every day, it seemed lately and funnel clouds, which people mistakenly called tornadoes, had become nuisances. He welcomed nature in all her moody forms, but the mobile was leaking where the kitchen and living room met, and the mildew smell was becoming something he couldn't ignore; he'd patched it up a few times, but water still settled behind the siding, festering there. Rattle didn't think much about the past on these walks, only the immediate future. The day ahead, as with most days – eggs, hash, painting, nap, roast beef sandwich (maybe toasted, maybe not), bike, club, beer, should-haves, head doctor's number on the nightstand ignored, younger body beside him ignored – would, if he was lucky, end in peaceful rest.

He watched two cardinals diving beneath branches and above the treetops. His newest fling, Irene, had asked what the tree and inky bird painted on his back meant, and he'd told her that from death comes life; he told the previous girlfriend it was about the connection of earth and sky. Two or three girlfriends back, he'd led someone to believe that the tattoo symbolized the slow growth of some folks and the ability of others to fly – this description was most accurate, but when he said it, her face dropped as though she were hoping for something more optimistic.

The redhead was faster than her labored breath suggested. She came up behind him just before he was able to finish the loop. As much as no one intimidated Rattle, the soft-bodied woman unsettled him. He made his way toward the mouth of the park, toward his bike, as she called out.

"You don't remember me?"

"Wrong guy," he said, not loud enough for her to hear.

"You visited me. I was only a kid then. I visited you when I was older. I hope for your sake that you don't remember. But, even if you do – even if you remember – I think we can talk now. I think you owe me that."

Rattle didn't remember, but he worried about what he might have done. A few years had been lost to him, and he knew he had no right to a relationship with his daughter now. He was surprised she didn't realize this.

No one could simply leave things be anymore; everyone had to look up everything and everyone else on the Internet, track them down, dissect their lives. The redhead, Elaine, was someone else's daughter, a girl who had been mailing him gushy and angry letters over the last two years, but who had been raised well. They shared DNA, but that was it.

Rattle wished he could feel something. Looking a little sore from the workout, she jogged toward him. "I knew it was you. I knew it. I hired help to find you; you know, you're off the grid, and I wasn't sure you were still alive. You look very alive. Why haven't you answered my mail, email?"

He knew she would follow him. He put on his helmet and began to kick up gravel as she trailed behind in a rusted Jeep. When the bike ground to a halt a mile from the park, on the corner of North Road and 22nd, he noticed she was hesitating, thinking of driving off probably, and he wished she would follow the impulse. She wiped her eyes and put on a ball cap before exiting her car. "This is where you live, eh?" she said.

"I live on my bike. This is where I stay."

"Those things terrify me. Is it a Harley?"

Rattle smiled with closed lips; his small teeth were rotting, something he often thought he'd go to Mexico to fix, then never did. "You get used to it," he mumbled. "And then you love it. And no, no, it is not. Come on, if you gotta."

"Glad you love *something*," she said, making her way toward the front door, hesitant but determined. Rattle noticed the way his trailer was sinking into the ground – something he could see all the clearer through her eyes.

"I'm not here to unload on you, so you know. I came because Mom died."

Rattle felt a pang as he brushed off a chair covered in a beige sheet and wondered how he should react. This sort of news never felt real when it arrived, yet if you didn't cry or crack in half from emotion, people thought you were cold. He said, "Sorry to hear. She was a good woman."

Elaine explained that the car accident had killed Josephine instantaneously. A truck had turned over, leaving three dead and one injured. "I heard the news report before I got the news, but I just knew that morning. I felt it coming."

She said she had inherited a little land that Josephine never mentioned, a dilapidated farmhouse in Marquette that she had renovated and was now teaching yoga in. She said she was alone but not lonely, that she had only been curious to meet him, and didn't want much of anything but maybe the sludgy instant coffee she was offered. He didn't volunteer anything about himself for the simple fact that there was nothing to tell.

Elaine was in pain right now, but she was doing well without him, better. And this was good, she was to remain elsewhere, flourishing, flying farther and farther from him so that he wouldn't burden her as he aged – that would be unfair. "You're a nice girl," he said. "I am not much for satisfying curiosity. I'm just surviving. The bike, the club, my routines – I'm alone too, but it's a good thing."

"A life like a movie, right? The cool-guy loner? The rebel?"

"It's not my movie," he said. Rattle poured a small pot of boiling water over a heap of crystalized dark coffee. Elaine watched him closely.

"Yeah, okay," she said. "Who wants responsibility?"

He remembered thinking about staying with Elaine's mother as he watched her stomach swell, but it was a smoother ride without her. She'd accused him of not feeling emotions like other people, called him a sociopath, which he worried was true. He'd convinced himself that if he impregnated a woman, he was contributing something, fulfilling his mission, and then he could leave. He wouldn't survive long for the world anyhow. He'd known that since he was a kid and his father died at 29. But the joke was on him; Rattle was alive and whole.

Elaine had written anger-edged letters before today; only one had been pleading. There were five in total. Most of the letters were addressed to the motorcycle club – the one thing he kept constant, and in a way he had enjoyed getting them, but he never imagined she'd show up in person. She was Josephine's kid through and through: thin nose, freckles dotting the apples of her cheeks. She asked him endless questions, such as why he didn't have a TV. "No time, no desire." Why didn't he have anything in the fridge? "Tend to eat at the club." Again: Why did he never write back?

After an uncomfortably long silence, Rattle offered his daughter more instant coffee. She wrote down the address of her new studio and told him it was nice to see him in person, that she liked his tattoos.

Rattle tried to sneak in, but the door to the farmhouse creaked. He saw a pile of red and gold pillows and grabbed one, placing it by the door.

Elaine's eyes didn't waver, didn't settle on him. He sat cross-legged and inhaled, almost choking on the spicy-sweet incense. He listened to her directions, focused on his third eye.

Since their meeting in the park, Elaine had written him twice. The first time, about a month after, she said she was pregnant and he should come meet her boyfriend, to which Rattle drank a fifth, and woke up in county. The second time, she said that her baby was due in a few months and her boyfriend had left. "Just like you." She was persevering, though, teaching yoga to mothers-to-be, and she had found a community in turn. She wrote that she would be having a natural birth, "though I'm sure you don't want to hear about that." She invited him to visit.

Rattle had not been able to take his eyes off her signature in this last letter. *Your daughter*, she'd written. It was a plea. In that same week, he had offered to help out on a parking lot rehab project and saved the extra money he earned to come visit.

Rattle breathed deeply, as instructed, attempting to relax his thoughts, watch them go by, but, inevitably, there was this nagging feeling that he had no way to make things right. *Sat Nam, in and out. Focus on the core. Focus on the strength, the life force. There is only now. No past. No future.* His body refused to soften.

Elaine taught the class how to breathe so deeply that the nourishment of oxygen would reach their toes, which would have been good for Rattle because his went numb from time to time, but he couldn't manage a breath that deep. The meditation was a full two hours today, a once-a-month deal, and he wasn't sure his legs were going to hold out like all these young women's did. His butt was propped up on a small red pillow, and there were a dozen other people sitting just like him in a stark room with large windows that looked out on a small garden with a sculpture of the Buddha in the middle next to a stone fountain. Breathe in: *Sat*, breathe out: *Nam*. Elaine told the class that yoga was the purest exercise in that it invites flow, thereby putting them all in touch with their true natures.

Despite the deep breaths, the peaceful room, the meditation seemed to wear on him. His thoughts were uncomfortable to watch. And with more than half an hour to go, he quit. Elaine had given them permission, a few times, to leave early if need be. "Everyone has limits."

Rattle glanced around at the room full of women. A few of them were watching as he shook his legs out and quietly walked to the door. It creaked again as he eased out. He felt an odd sensation at his back, something like pin pricks – as though his tattoos were still being carved, and that feeling eased some with the fresh air. When he lit a cigarette, however, it returned and shot down his arms. That head doctor he went to one time said it was probably psychosomatic; all the emotions he couldn't face were being internalized, manifesting themselves into physical pain.

"All illness is either guilt or longing," she'd said. He decided he wouldn't talk to her after that.

All guilt is useless, he told himself, countering the psychologist's theory with his mother's. He'd stolen a Cadbury Easter egg, the kind with the milky middle that looked like a real egg, when he was seven. The guilt of it made his stomach hurt so badly that he couldn't enjoy the egg, so he confessed the next morning over grits. "Guilt is useless," she'd said. "Snap the fuck out of it. Now eat your grits and give me that candy. I love them things." She smacked him then, palm to temple, hard enough to render splitting pain for days and seal her advice. Willing himself to feel nothing, he lay on the floor as he had so many times that day,

He and his mother shared the same inclinations, he thought now. He could give life but not nurture it. He smoked four hand-rolled cigarettes and sat, shirtless, out front, until he heard Elaine's voice. *Sat Nam*, she said, approaching him – all round shapes and red-orange hair. She had a mat rolled up under her arm, and she paused to say her goodbyes to the stream of women walking to their cars. These women smiled at Rattle, but did not stare or look in awe; they looked at Elaine with pure admiration. He stared back, close-mouthed, as he had at least four construction gigs' worth of dental work to be done – the constant pain, he could live with, but he couldn't stomach the embarrassment in front of what seemed Elaine's congregation.

"The tattoo of the tree and the bird," she said. "That me?"

His heart began to thrust toward his ribcage, and he repositioned as he answered. "Yeah, that's you."

Elaine looked slantwise; her face went blurry; Rattle felt a surge of liquid metal spread throughout his chest. He wondered if he'd been shot, and he tried to look around, but his neck was stiff atop his wilting body, and before he knew it, he was on the ground.

Months passed before Rattle returned to the park. A mild heart attack, the doctors had said, and Elaine remained by his side, visiting daily. When he became strong enough, he reminded her that she had to think about her own life. "You have a business to run, so go on. Get. I've been through worse. I'll call the club."

The air, ever since the attack, felt anything but fresh. It became thick and sticky, and he cut across the path, heading to the street. Endless rows of corn led him and left him. His hips ached. *Regret is useless*, he reminded himself; nonetheless, he felt it there —something hard beneath his skin. His days had become longer, the walks no longer peaceful. Elaine messaged him when the baby was born. She said she would love for him to be a part of the girl's life, but she wouldn't force it. A picture of a pink-cheeked girl with green eyes and an indignant expression made Rattle chuckle a little.

He kept all of Elaine's letters in a large dark basket that he'd picked up at the thrift store. He read them all that night with whiskey, then with beer. He read them again and again. He read them the next morning, over eggs. He put them in order from angry to sad, and started with angry, trying to feel something in return. He couldn't, or so he told himself, as his fragile heart swelled behind his ribs.

Dear Elaine, I'm an empty old man, he wrote at the top of a piece of notebook paper. He thought awhile, then added, *That emptiness stops with you.* He was proud of this line, felt it somewhat poetic for a guy who hadn't even finished freshman year of high school. He would add more to it and mail it tomorrow, he thought, stumbling to get another beer, but instead, it sat there. After work each day, he'd go to CVS and stand beneath the vent reading every single new baby greeting card, only to buy a pack of Nicorette or some pretzels instead.

Rattle began walking the loop three times a day. He barely noticed anymore when people stopped or stared at him. He found enough work to occupy daylight hours, stayed busy with masonry and construction – anything he could find. He saved everything he could that summer to pay down his hospital bill and found a dentist who would fit him with dentures and not lecture him about not going for the last ten years or flossing enough. After five seasons of taking every job he could, he packed his clothes, filling two trash bags and a backpack, and he set out to meet his granddaughter and find work closer to his daughter. It was a journey and a new start, and he felt much like he used to feel, with a pretty girl and a cold sixer in the bike storage – only, this time, he was an old man with tired eyes and fading tattoos.

He pulled up the bike and sat by an oak tree, watching a mother jog down the street with a stroller. He noticed how pristine the neighborhood was, how much trouble these people must go through to keep such perfect lawns. His legs were still vibrating as he walked to the door. He felt the weight of his age and the weakening of electricity in his veins. There was a toy lawnmower outside the door that would blow bubbles if pushed. He knocked, running his tongue over his new teeth.

Elaine's eyes were flat when she opened the door; he wondered what he must look like to her now. He'd brought the letter, but his granddaughter was, what, a year old now? Older? He handed Elaine a small gold locket for the baby, whose name, she said, was Jane. "We call her Janie."

She didn't look at the engraved message. In fact, Elaine blocked the doorway like a bouncer. Just beyond her, he could make out child-proof plug coverings and the corner of a crib, where two little feet in pink and white socks jerked around as though dancing. The pain and joy blasted his bones. The feeling was both restorative and deserved.

"I existed for you," he wanted to tell Elaine. Instead, he handed her what he'd written and waited for her to speak.

She bowed her head. "Never knowing when you'll respond or show up. I don't want Janie to go through it." She paused, but couldn't bear the silence. "You look healthy, though, and I'm so glad for that. I just can't – rather, I don't have the energy to keep reaching out. How about you do the reaching, and if you can do that, then we'll let you in. How about that?"

Just after Janie's second birthday, Elaine decided that the girl deserved to see her

163

grandfather, if only once. Janie was as tall as Elaine's hip now, and she stood gripping her mother's belt loop, as a woman named Mrs. Johnson, who lived a mile from Rattle's old trailer, said, "Yeah, I saw him about a year ago. He said something about returning to the island, then sped away westward down N Road on that loud bike, unsettling all kinds of gravel. I hate those bikes. He was headed toward the sunset like he was in a damn movie or something. Haven't seen him since." She dropped a cigarette and put it out with her bare heel.

Elaine thanked Mrs. Johnson and glanced down the road, the way her father had headed. She imagined him somewhere in a small tattoo shop, spending his hard-earned money on more ink, marking all the places he'd been, so he didn't have to bother with the memories. She imagined how much the needle must hurt as it pierced the skin. She lifted Janie, and those soft, chubby arms settled around her neck as the two of them headed east.

FORTUNE IN SMOKE

The waters are calmer on the other side of the island, down that hill toward all the resorts. This is the windy side, an untouched beachfront. You can see the whitecaps for miles. The waves are as violent as they are stunning though – you should know these things.

These are the iron shores, so you want to jump out from that platform toward the mouth of the keyhole, straight out, if you *must* swim. Beach shoes are necessary, unless you don't mind the bottoms of your feet cut all to hell, and don't go out if you aren't a strong swimmer.

Since your interest is in Casa Luna, and we are so happy to have you, there are things you should know. There are always winds like these. Feel them fully, breathe in the sounds, and allow your pores to swell with ocean air.

Don't worry about blow dryers or shaving. The switches will work again soon; the blackouts are rolling. We have a generator, but there are hiccups. Sorry we didn't mention that online. Oh, and your smartphones won't work, but there are track phones and phone cards you can buy at a shop down the hill. It will be open on Monday.

You might want to retire those cameras while I show you around. If everything is a postcard or a selfie, experiences are reduced to background. Besides, there will be time later. Plenty of it, I assure you. Live and breathe the beauty. It *is* striking, yes.

In '98, Hurricane Mitch delivered bodies to the shore, right where you're standing now. Oh, no need to move – just a little history. Infant-sized jeans and ravaged dresses, button-eyed dolls and counting games, washed up from the mainland for years after that storm. There is a well-preserved music box in your room, in fact, which arrived snug in a suitcase. The music is faint, but it still plays.

It was shortly after the storm first hit that Luna arrived. Luna, as in *Casa de*, yes. She was one of seven survivors who came from another, smaller island that you can almost see on a clear day. They arrived by boat. Others arrived piece by piece, wave by wave, not so lucky.

At night, you will sometimes see lights there, against the brush. They are brighter than you'll expect, will appear broad and round as though from flashlights. That's her, searching. We moved the house.

No, she's not a ghost. Nothing so simple. She's a piece of the island. She's a part of the natural world. Hers is just one story of many. If you're looking to stay here, you should know at least one. You would like to hear it? I am happy to share.

That area, beyond the coconut trees, is where the original house stood. Luna squatted there when she first arrived, along with her two cousins. This was a private beach even then, and all of the homes belonged to an American woman who showed face maybe once a year. Luna was inspired that a woman owned all this, the whole compound. She set out to meet her, in hopes of finding mentorship, possibly partnership. She wanted to make a good impression, so she began visiting the primary schools, sitting in the small chairs, listening, and jotting notes.

Luna would stand at the fork at the bottom of the hill, all the way down there, and take short, staccato puffs on an oversized cigar she offered around. The only woman to smoke cigars in this area, she was known for this. A group of people waited for rides to the beach to work then; she was one of many who hopped on truck beds and banged on the backs of clouded windows when a turn signal suggested the wrong way. They'd do the same down there, near Foster's beachfront, and then again at night until they reached this very fence here.

A year after Luna's arrival, the owner visited to meet a contractor and oversee work on a property. Luna was nervous. She'd practiced what she'd say. She wore a friend's church clothes and put away her cigars, as she knew they dampened her image to Americans. She introduced herself, stood tall, and offered to take care of the land in exchange for the space and wages. She assured the woman that she had a great deal of respect for her, and suggested that her family would keep the grounds as well as anyone could.

The woman agreed, with some reluctance, but ultimately never paid the living wage promised. As months and then years passed, Luna and her cousins restored the home as best they could. At first gratefully, then resentfully. Their work was worth more.

The cousins did construction, and Luna gave massages on the beach. Tourist massages were big business then, as now, when people like you began to arrive with curious eyes and knotted shoulders. Luna worked long days kneading flesh, spent her nights drinking and making friends.

She wrote to the landowner with updates, regularly asking if she could buy a piece of the land, pay it off slowly. But her requests were either ignored or waylaid with contingencies.

It was around this time that Luna began to have visions.

She told everyone she massaged that she could see beyond the day for them, far beyond. No one believed her at first. She continued to foretell, however, and after so many correct predictions, there was no denying her accuracy. She made powerful friends by telling fortunes, was invited to parties with government officials as an act, and then as a friend. She got legal advice, negotiated for papers.

After putting so much work into the land, after making the right friends, Luna decided she deserved what she deserved. She had a pseudo deed created and claimed ownership of the land from there – on that hill – to here, where you will be staying tonight. This island, whose roads had become the veins through which her blood flowed, who had welcomed her to its shores, was as much hers by this time as anyone's. And the woman, the previous landowner she had once respected, was now nothing more than a leech on her new land.

Luna's fortune-telling business grew so fast that almost everyone on the island came to know and either admire or fear her. She gave up massage and shared her visions full-time, rarely having to leave her property.

If Luna predicted death, there would be death. Good fortune meant an imminent windfall. Some speculated that she orchestrated these events, ensuring that her fortunes rang true by employing family and friends to carry them out.

But only conspiracy theorists, such as my grandfather, thought this way, and he knew better than to share his theory. Luna began to curse or bless, depending on need, becoming a spiritual figure to some. Eventually she cashed in on this by claiming she could not only see the future but alter it – for a price.

A haunting story, yes. But it doesn't end so well.

Luna was still injured by that hurricane, rattled by nightmares of the day she lost her husband. She longed for the child she'd had only nine months prior to that horrendous storm.

Her loss returned to her late in life. It carved lines into her face, encircling her eyes, and tilting her mouth toward the earth. She would still clutch her sheets upon hearing a particularly strong wind; she still found remnants of life lost, reminders of her own survival washed up on shore. But during the waking hours, she wore strength like fine clothing.

She heaved in smoke as she looked out at the waves, breath of fire, and she blew hard, tracing shapes into the gray cloud to seal her fortunes or dole them out. The smoke didn't lie, but with too little sleep or after a squabble with her cousins, her fortunes became tainted and darkened. After a time, it seemed that if Luna was in a bad mood, her customers would pay the ultimate price.

Elfie, a neighbor, was the only person to publicly accuse Luna of witchcraft. The instant she said so, her fortune could be seen flickering out. All it took was a long stare from Luna to unhinge the woman's mind. Everyone told her to watch out, and so she did. She stopped leaving her cabana, refused to walk along the beach as she used to, then avoided the lobster nights and rum she once lived for.

Without her routines, Elfie lost her light. She lost her mind. She'd wander around in the brush and mutter to herself. It was Elfie who set Luna's house ablaze, which killed her mid-nightmare. We all knew. Luna's revenge would not rise up in the smoke and flame but soon appear in the very ocean that had brought her here.

While Luna had destroyed Elfie's mind, it was guilt that wore on her heart. She began to have palpitations, then took a spill. She saw things, as though Luna's visions had transferred to her. When she saw boats sinking, none of the deep-sea fishermen came home. When she saw blades, murder rates doubled.

The rains were not strong, but they were persistent; they caused enough cumulative damage that it was as though the island had been hit by a major storm. Something happened every holiday – lost power at the grocery, a sudden collective rot of fruit. The church's roof fell in twice.

The winds started to pick up on this side of the island shortly after Luna's death, and I doubt they will settle again. Legend has it that every person who drowned that year, a record number, saw lights like those I described just before the waves would swallow them.

Look down there, way down. There will be development this time next year, six condos and a garish pool full of chlorine right next to this angry ocean. There will be more visiting, people with bright-colored straws, candy-colored porches, and homes built to rent.

Our island is etching itself into a new psyche, a wrinkle deepening in the collective brain. Our island has destroyed and been destroyed. Its people have sought education and have become investors – though not in large enough numbers.

The resorts are beautiful, they bring in the money, but they stomp on the magic as well as the coral, so I ask you to be respectful during your stay.

There are more stories. I can tell you one for every lot, every day. You stay long enough, or come enough times, and you'll hear all that I know to tell. You'll hear the ocean in your dreams. You'll see Luna, and she'll see you.

You look frightened, but please don't be. If you're afraid, you're not listening. Luna is nature now. She warns us when she can, so you can snorkel and zipline and do all the touristy things you've come to do. The island will tell all. It will embed its stories beneath your skin, and I won't need to tell you to come again. You will put down those bags and carry the whole of it with you when you leave.

Look at that! We have light. Let's go get that mocha you saw online at our new café near

West Bay. I'll show you the calm waters after, the other side of the island. I'll show you what you saw in the pictures.

I see you have your cameras poised. I suppose you should do what you'd like. Later, you must go to lobster night and imbibe sugary rum and dance next to coconut trees. This is, after all, your vacation.

THE SHAPE OF LOSS

> "When the blackbird flew out of sight,
> It marked the edge
> Of one of many circles."
>
> —Wallace Stevens, "Thirteen Ways
> of Looking at a Blackbird"

Jackson ignored the knocking and gave his coffee a few slow stirs. After rinsing the single-serve filter, he shook his hands dry and listened to the doorbell chime. He counted to five as his eyes settled on the orange and yellow lights, an abstract painting of Bourbon Street on a black-blue night. The sky was textured, but there were no stars.

Chris had just turned seven the year she picked out the painting after deliberating over a dozen or so that all looked the same to Jackson. He remembered leaning on the counter near the cash register, watching as his young wife crouched with their daughter to help, and offering suggestions that were promptly dismissed. In the end, Chris chose the one with the darkest sky and brightest streetlights. "I like the contrast," she surmised. The shop owner patted Jackson on the back then. "Contrast! What a concept for a little girl."

She would've grown up with the gift of artistic understanding, a thing Jackson was readying himself to envy. Taking bitter sips of black coffee – he usually took milk but hadn't bothered with the grocery this week – his eyes shifted so that he could see the woman's shadow, soft and short, outside. She was knocking now.

He imagined her shadow morphing: thinning, elongating, and hunching slightly forward. He could see it becoming smaller, rounder, and unable to stay still. The woman moved at last, and her shadow disappeared from view. The phone began ringing. Jackson saw her peering in the window one last time before turning to leave. Mercifully, he answered the door.

"Hello, Mr. Waters?" Jackson nodded. "It is a pleasure to finally meet you. I was beginning to think I had the wrong house, or that you didn't exist. People say that you don't, you know." She smiled, waited for a response. Had Jackson been a kind man, he'd have said something like, "Well here I am, myth and legend." But instead, he let her squirm.

She was a short woman, as her shadow had suggested, and she had a crop of hair that was light brown and lightened to blonde in thin streaks around her face. She straightened her shoulder strap and waited for an invitation inside. Jackson led her to his office.

"Your home is immaculate!" she said. Jackson said nothing. He had three spreadsheets open on two screens in his office. He was always working. He gestured toward them as Olga examined the room. "You have a lovely home," she tried again.

Jackson counted to ten; he could do this. Indulge her. Be a gentleman. He said, "Thank you. As you can see, growth rates are stable but steadily declining in the market over the next two years, the short-term as we define it for the purpose of this study, and it is my job to find opportunities for this client; more specifically, to find data that will shift the down arrow up, and it is an impossible task. It boils down to integrity."

"Yes, Mr. Waters. I understand your position can be challenging."

To Jackson, Olga's words were visible, coming out of her mouth in precise, rounded shapes that slowly disappeared as they made their way toward him. His ability to visualize so precisely had served his career well over the years. His specialty was measurements and instrumentation, micro technologies, but he was a mathematician at heart. He knew the micro machinery market more intimately than anyone, could see the data formulating and extending itself long before his computer could catch up. He was the go-to if companies had questions about the way multiple sensors worked within intricate machinery, and he consulted when new functionalities were introduced. He knew the mechanical ecosystem inside and out. He saw the inner workings of everything and, so he thought, everyone.

But clients wanted him to fabricate, exaggerate, and he couldn't stomach them. His boss wanted him to present at trade shows and travel the world – a thing he used to do when he had a family; choices that made him physically ill to think about now, so many choices to be away for work. He resented his job, his boss, himself.

Every year during his review, Mr. Martin extended restrained praise, asked him to offer trainings at the office, asked that he go to Europe a few weeks. Jackson had always said yes, but now that he was alone and had every reason in the world to go, he couldn't leave the house. He couldn't leave the painting of Bourbon Street. He couldn't leave for fear that he'd return and forget the stories of things.

No, mistakes had been made, and now Jackson was content to stay put in his little corner of the Midwest in a solitary home office where he could actually get things done. Mike, one of the junior statisticians Jackson spoke to via Zoom on Fridays, told him that the newer employees speculated he was actually a robot or that there was a team of underpaid specialists out of the Iskandar office doing the job under the umbrella of Jackson Waters. He never showed face at functions or holiday parties. He never showed face unless he was on assignment.

This year, Olga was making the trip in place of the yearly phone call with Mr. Martin. She was the result of an initiative to improve employee relations. Jackson had been told she was also working for HR. In other words, she would be firing, determining fate. She shifted on his stiff office chair—the one he never used. The one that had been abandoned since Deb used to sit there and work the crossword or practice her vocal exercises as Jackson worked, quick to ask him for answers to questions she knew he'd know. She indulged him like that and probably didn't realize he noticed. He loved her for it.

"This is a lovely chair. Is it vintage?" she asked.

"Probably," Jackson said, noting that this was the second time she used lovely, a word with a wide shape that moves inward, hits like a soft punch. Lovely was too formal and inaccurate a word for that chair, he thought. Deb had been lovely, her chair a throne.

His stomach grumbled. He wanted this woman out of his house. He counted to twenty, thinking, organizing his thoughts. "Can we do this elsewhere?" he asked at last.

He suggested Phil's on 14th Street, a place he'd ordinarily go to sit in a tattered red booth by the window and eat two eggs over-easy, a glut of hash browns, and inch-thick rye toast with strawberry jam most Sundays. This was the closest he'd come to an excursion, grocery shopping after and running simple errands. Phil's had, at one time, been a regular family outing after hikes or soccer practice.

Olga looked hesitant but said, "Sure. Restroom?"

He pointed down the hall. As he put his computer to sleep and slid his chair under the desk, he heard a swooshing sound and turned to find all of Olga's papers scattered across the dark wood floor. He imagined her in there staring at the hairbrush and barrettes left out on the sink. They'd been there since the accident.

As he shuffled the papers back into a pile, his stomach grumbled like an old coffee maker. He could hear the water flowing from the sink as he spotted his name, Jackson Waters, with a red outline on it. Most of the names had green or yellow, and he knew what red meant. He saw a write-up in his file in response to his request for leave.

Plane accident on August 16, Q4, 2015 verified. Notes: The accident was highly publicized. Deborah Waters was a newscaster on Channel 4. Employee took only a few days bereavement. Refused counseling or additional time off. Productivity did not suffer, but other behaviors are concerning. Client complaint in Q1 about inattentive manner. Vendor and important client (see complaints and feedback file 344) mentioned without closing project or altering business. Recommendations: Performance Improvement Plan (PIP). One year probation to ensure employee is able to fulfill tasks.

There was far more, but this was enough. When the door opened, Jackson was waiting with a neat pile of papers. "Your files fell out. You might want to put them back in order as we head there. I'll drive," he said. He noticed Olga was wearing fresh lipstick now, a dark pink color unnatural to anything save a flower.

Shelly, a petite woman who taught jazz on the weekends and had, at one time, been Chris's instructor, greeted them with a smile. She wore white tights and red shoes on a black and white checkered floor. "Hey, Jackson. Didn't beat the rush today, eh?"

The rush comprised twelve people between the tables and bar. Jackson said, "Hi, Shelly. Two today."

"Good, good. Got y'all. Follow me. You know, we have a new pancake today, a peanut butter and chocolate pancake that we make with whole wheat flour." She smiled widely and waited for them to react. "You know, whole wheat for balance." She laughed a little. Her laugh made her sound like a seal, a wet hand rubbing a balloon. She was always kind to Jackson but never pried when the news was citywide and the rest of Toledo seemed intent on pitying looks and inane questions such as, "How have you been doing?" All she'd said is, "I'll miss them," then left it alone.

"Pancakes with peanut butter. No, wait, eggs," Olga said with a warm voice and cool eyes. Jackson kept forgetting she was there. He was so used to being alone. She clutched her files tight to her side as though fearful they would again expose her. They both asked for coffee with cream, no sugar, to start.

After placing his file folder on the table, Olga told Jackson about the company's new agenda to become more involved in employees' lives. She sounded like a recording, spouting company-approved lingo and tempered optimism with the requisite threatening undercurrent. She said this initiative was part of a trend among high-performing corporations.

She explained everything as Jackson listened to both her and the rest of the restaurant, taking in the concert of atmosphere: Quarterly numbers were not as great, but as you know this tends to be the case Q2...these eggs are runny, gross, look...the initiative is based on a triangular model of optimization. That waitress has a nice ass...stop teasing your brother...after some resistance...and then she told him she was married...has already proven successful as proven by numerous studies...you make it to the pork festival last weekend? Bet they're still using the bacon...year-over-year sales performance...team player...margins, margins...here you are, and would you like ketchup? Sugar-free syrup?

Jackson slapped the table to break the sound. "Formality is a waste of time, and you sound like you're reading from index cards. I'm on a performance plan; I saw that when you dropped my file, and you'll be back in six months. Got it." Her face was a pale square, her rehearsed words: rectangles that feel, inconsequentially, to the floor.

Olga cleared her throat. "Quite frankly, Mr. Waters, we cannot continue to overlook your lack of vision in the future of the company. The nature of the micro-machinery business is volatile and, accordingly, we need timely research and analysis that is willing to bend logic today to find the logic of tomorrow. More importantly, we need happy clients. Do you understand? Our clients are forward-thinking, and our deliverables must meet expectations in order to maintain accounts and attract new clients. We cannot forecast to five years anymore. We must forecast twenty years, twenty-five. These are the topics we've been covering in our weekly meetings, and we see you have not attended virtually as requested."

"Bend logic in order to find the logic of the future?" Jackson said as Olga's scrambled eggs were placed before her. "Fuck you. How about that logic?"

Jackson decided that when she stormed out, he would finish his breakfast and stop for cream before heading home. He was dressed for it, and maybe it would clear his mind. Olga was sitting toward the edge of the booth. Another person could easily be positioned next to her. His daughter with her chocolate chip pancakes and uncanny ability to balance the salt shaker in a tiny mound of salt.

Olga didn't move, didn't waver. He needed this job. He had bills, a mortgage. He got regular settlement checks from the airline, but he didn't want that money, tore each month's check into eight even parts that he'd ceremoniously flush down the toilet, watching them swell and swirl.

"Quality is something you have pride in. I am here to recommend a course in near-future employment. When we give clients favorable results, they lend themselves to more similar results. It's about being future focused. You work hard, and that is what is expected every time. So let's just have a chat about where you see yourself in the future of the company," Olga continued.

"Did you hear me say fuck you?" he asked. "Let's not bullshit clients. Let's tell them the truth."

"I'm here to help to guide you. The company wouldn't send me here if they didn't want to retain you."

"Retain?"

"Retain, Mr. Waters. Are you ready to talk now?" Her cheeks reddened for the first time as she paused. Her tone shifted. "You know, this is my first time in Toledo, or Ohio, for that matter."

Jackson sopped up yolk with a toasted piece of rye, noting Olga shifting in her seat, edging closer to the middle. He watched as she pressed her napkin against her white toast to sop up some of the butter. A blackbird flew into the window beside them, which made a loud smack. They looked outside to find the bird flying toward them again, head-planting, thwacking against the glass.

"They do that because they see their reflection," Jackson said.

"We need to stop this," Olga said, tapping the glass, then knocking on it.

This woman was the opposite of Debbie, who had rarely worn makeup, or noticeable makeup, outside of work. She often complained that they slathered her in the stuff before she went on air, and her skin needed to breathe. "I feel like I'm made of plastic when I wear all that," she would say, kicking off her heels and clearing her space. She jogged but never turned down a piece of cake, she played Scrabble with the kid for hours, said she'd soon give up caffeine every day as she drank her coffee. Debbie lived in comfort and offered it in turn.

"Radiant," he used to whisper as he combed her hair with his fingers, when she complained about the station, which wanted her to lose five pounds or get a mini-lift or shoot her face with poison. She was going to quit soon. She'd always wanted to write instead.

"I'm going to recommend you return to the office," Olga said, interrupting his thoughts and reassuming her matter-of-fact tone. She appeared plastic, a middle-aged Barbie, a smattering of paints and dyes and tricks. She was tired beneath her mask though; she kept glancing outside. The bird was perched in a tree across the street, likely stunned. Jackson stared at it as he responded.

"Nope. You might as well fire me." He ate his last few bites of potatoes with pepper, took measured bites as she stared out the window at the bird, too. He knew the company didn't want to lose him. He could imagine Olga getting orders to come up with a result, to change his behavior but not let him go.

"I hate my job," Olga said, rubbing her index finger against a small patch of scars on her upper cheek. He hadn't noticed them before. He wondered what it would be like to lean over the table and hold the back of her head, pull her toward him, to kiss those scars gently. He then became sick with the thought and took a long drink of icy water.

"You seem good at it," he said.

"I feel like a reaper. I don't feel like I'm doing any – any one thing of value, just telling people to do better and sign papers. I'm walking red tape. I determine the monetary value of people for a company." Her words tugged at his chin, lifted him from the booth. Jackson imagined pushing the ceramic plates from the table and tucking his foot behind her stockinged knee. He imagined Debbie telling him to go ahead, that she wanted him to reconnect with the world, too, with anyone in the world.

Olga looked him in the eyes for the first time, and he felt shaky. He wouldn't know Olga's story but imagined she touched that tender place of honesty for a reason, maybe because she figured he'd barely register it. She must've thought him insane and, for some reason, this made her feel safe.

He counted to thirty. He'd be up to a hundred by day's end. He counted when he needed to reorient, to engage. He'd had to do it when working occasionally but more often when interacting.

"I understand," Jackson said, actually moving his foot around her leg, actually leaning in to test the reality of the situation, his imagination invaded reality. Small talk, he told himself. "Do you like San Francisco? You are based there, I assume."

"Um." She pressed her leg into his foot. "Yes, it's lovely. I'd rather live somewhere quaint like this though, less driving." She glanced outside again, and her cheeks drained, her face fell. "If you won't come back to office, you're fired. I have direct orders."

"Quaint is one way to look at this town."

Something broke in the kitchen, and a small girl jumped up on the booth behind theirs to peer beyond Jackson. A woman began to tickle her, and she slid back down into her seat. Chris had been an adult before her time, not the kind of girl to jump up on a booth seat, though she would've wanted to investigate. She would've glanced over at the kitchen doors, maybe tell Jackson something along the lines of, "Someone will be paying for that!" Jackson would nod, tell her he was thinking the same.

"Look, Mr. Waters, I can't tell you what to do," Olga went on, "but I would recommend going to the office, to get out of your routine. Doing something. You're good at what you do, you need a nudge. I say that unofficially. I say it because I've lost someone, too."

"A nudge." Jackson pushed his plate away, glanced outside. Watching the street with a tilted head, the blackbird was perched on a higher, thinner branch, calm now. Another bird joined it, and there was ruffling and rippling of feathers.

"I'm going to quit, Jackson," she said, "as soon as I find something better, so I can be very honest here. And yes, a nudge." There was no shape to her words, but there was truth. Loss was nothing more than absence – he lived inside of absence. Their legs intertwined. Hers were stockinged and strong.

"I work at home because it's quiet," he said. "The Toledo office is tiny and loud. I work at home because my family still lives there, through the things that surround me."

"Don't sign then. Did you hear what I said? I don't really care. You can live however you'd like, and the company can pay for our breakfast, and we can move on. Both of us. Whatever. I think, however, as a person with no right to say this, as a mere observer, you need to change something."

He reached for the paperwork. "Maybe I'm going to quit too, he said." He counted to forty, he counted to fifty; his stomach tingled as though gravity had just caught up. The counting was a technique a therapist had taught him. It centered him. Visualizing words made them seem more objective. These were his tricks.

The blackbirds danced and fought and flew, traced the edge of invisible circles. The restaurant bustled. Their legs were pressed at the thigh.

The two shook hands over the table and wished each other the best with requisite formality, but their hands – soft, cool –locked tighter when they should have released, remained intertwined long enough to silence the background and tell of a future with a different slope. They scooted out from the tattered booth and paid for the check with a company credit card. For the first time in a long time, Jackson wasn't ready to go home.

THE SLOPE OF A LINE

So many mistakes. The heaviest of them rests on Rattle's thighs and flattens its palms against his shoulders. He hears the rush on the freeway nearby, remembers raging down 315 at criminal speeds. He was sinewy and strong then, steering the straight line. Asking about his travels, people greeted him by name in clubs from Toledo to Cincinnati, his parents had never set foot out of Ohio, had barely ventured out of the old Victorian rooming house they shared with a rotation of renters.

Today, Rattle is hooked up to tubes and beeping machines in a room with a moaning roommate and the non-stop noise of a flat-screen. He lives compartmentally: rest and forced interactions with dry-eyed, over-sanitized nurses who serve him spongy, beige foods. All of the nurses look tired except one – an over-attentive young man who calls himself Sandy, whose nametag says *Sanderson*, who is currently knocking on the door as he opens it.

"Hello, gentlemen," he says. "Lovely morning today, absolutely lovely. Would you like me to open the blinds?" Rattle doesn't answer. The roommate grunts, turning over as much as possible to face the wall. For all his moaning, this roommate will be fine. He had gallbladder surgery and will be released in a day or two. For all his moaning, he is not the one in this room who will soon die. His family, a wife and kid, visits daily; sometimes the kid throws Rattle a casual smile, which he absorbs like sunlight.

Sandy eases open the blinds, pausing briefly in case of protest, but Rattle welcomes the lines of warmth on his multi-colored skin. Many of his tattoos are fading, now a greenish gray, especially the number 18 penned jaggedly on his thigh, a gang symbol, a mere mark – least significant to his life and most problematic. Others are holding up. He blinks his eyes in the light-washed room.

Rattle is actively dying, feeling every sensory shift more acutely than he had the day before. He'd planned on being buried long ago, on an island off the coast of Honduras, but due to the unexpected accumulation of years, even decades, he will die here in Columbus, Ohio, where every road sign points toward a world that puts Midwestern agonies in perspective.

He has slow, deep stomach bleeding that cannot be stopped, was supposed to be moved to hospice yesterday, but is headed there today instead. He is on pain medications that rival those he used to crave, only he feels no high and no relief; he feels only the shutting down of machinery.

"I want to write my own obit," Rattle tells Sandy.

"Then write it," he says, handing Rattle a pen.

Rattle will be survived by two people he selfishly considers his children, Alex and Elaine, and neither will know till after. Alex is not blood, but he is Rattle's son nonetheless. The boy, for his part, wouldn't come anyhow. The boy is lost, somewhere in San Pedro Sula, trying to create a sturdy life on shaky ground. Elaine is here in Ohio;

she'd reached out so many – too many – times before Rattle was incarcerated.

He never wrote to her. Rather, he had, but the letters were never mailed. He was fearful of the secrets in his bloodline, worried about his influence on her and, one day, her daughter. His absence was his greatest gift to her. Rattle had seen his granddaughter once. She was a plump little bundle swathed in pink and white, whose eyes surveyed the room that day and seemed to settle on everything but him.

Rattle opens his eyes, as though to see if he can. The pen has been removed from his grip and placed on the side table. Sandy saunters into the bathroom and then out; the scarf around his neck tucked neatly into his scrubs is an odd comfort. A patient made him this scarf, said he reminded her of her grandson.

"Nod off there, Snake Man?" Sandy asks with a half-smile. He reaches for the scarf when Rattle looks up, to ensure it is secure and in place. There is a glimmer to it, some sparkly strings woven into the edges that catch the light and dance along the shadows. "They'll be coming in to get you soon."

"Wait. Did I sign the papers that say you won't keep me alive for no reason?" Rattle asks.

"You did. We're taking you somewhere more comfortable. Like I promised, remember?"

"If you're lying, I'll come back and haunt you." Rattle's voice sounds plucked, reverberating in a hesitant way. When he arrived, it had still been strong and low, soft but intent.

"You think people don't threaten me with that on a daily basis?" Sandy says. "I have a ghost entourage."

"How can one man fuck up so many times in his life and make it this far?" Rattle asked Sandy last Friday, a day that celebrated his eightieth with yet another talk about surgery – when there was still hope – and a smuggled-in cupcake from Sandy, which, Rattle was pretty sure, had enough THC in it to put an elephant in catatonic shock.

"An outlier, almost ten years over the average of a healthy man." For bikers, eighty is damn near double the average. For men in prison, for smokers, for red-meat eaters, for people with no close relationships, for those with a history of addiction – he's an outlier, all right, but he can't tease out the reason.

"The good die young," Rattle suggests.

"Original theory you got there." Sandy waves the dying man's comment off and crouches down to add, "You'll like our comfortable unit, doll. You'll like it much better. Better company."

"Better, as in none?"

When he closes his eyes, sleep washes over him. Dreams come rapidly, as though they've been ready to pounce. Sleep consumes most days now. Some days his dreams feel nearer to reality than wakefulness. In dreams, it is easier to breathe; he sees his children.

He often dreams of the past, memories like film that bends. His children are shadows, running toward him. The world is a Dali painting, and Rattle stands on time.

Rattle falls back to consciousness, to pain. Sandy is now gone, and the room is warmer; it has two windows, the feel of a cottage. There is a burnt-orange wall to his left, a couch and a chair by one window where he can gaze out. No roommate, no groaning, no beeping.

Each blink comes with sleep now, and the dreams blend with reality. He can make out the fuzzy lines of a shape by the window. Whoever is sitting there is hunching forward, looking into open palms. Rattle falls into a world where he could still hop on his motorcycle, where he is fully alive, hair blowing behind him, the wind rapping against his face and loosening the skin on his arms.

The slope of a line determines a trajectory; Rattle's descent is steep, and he dreams of rapping on Elaine's door; he sees his granddaughter again, a tiny bundled thing wrapped up like a package. His daughter, angling herself in the doorway, becoming a wall, a barrier; he sees Alex, calling him *Father*, then nodding, losing himself in drink, becoming a wall.

When he wakes to find Sandy gently dabbing up the sweat from his forehead, he searches for the time.

"You were shaking, dear. Sandy's got you now."

He doesn't understand why it's taking so long. "Why am I still here?"

Some patients get to Sandy. His mother had been a nurse, able to put up a barrier made up of detached niceties, which allowed her to deliver bad news, pierce the skin, replace an IV bag, wipe away blood speckles from the cheeks and chests of lung-damaged cancer patients. She'd taught him to insist they call him by a different name, to create an alter ego. "Think of yourself as a sort of superhero," she'd told him. "We usher people to health, and sometimes, oftentimes in our unit, we usher them toward the next world." He'd lost the ability to see himself this way when he'd lost her, but he always tried.

This patient, who asked Sandy to call him *Rattle* – the embodiment of ego armament – had collapsed in a mall seven days ago, a warm oatmeal cookie in his hand, his body covered in tattoos. He collapsed again behind the wheel, lost control. When a truck hit, his insides crammed together in an unsolvable puzzle. He occupied Room 402 for three days because community hospice was full. He's been in and out of consciousness since.

Sandy visits today in the still, small room, with its warm paints and pumpkin smells. This is not Sandy's unit, but he is here because he has to be. There is something about this patient – the tough guy, the vulnerability, the apology. Maybe it's just the fact that he has no one else.

Sandy imagines his own father, the lack of remorse for never being what he was meant to be, and he imagines how much it must weigh on a person at the end – that armor. For some reason, it makes Sandy all the more compassionate toward this man. "It is not the children who miss out," his mother used to tell him.

"So many mistakes," the patient says again, his voice a poetic whisper, his body a vaguely familiar collage. The patient's blood is releasing slowly, filling his organs, but with the pain meds, there is little physical anguish. So Sandy is told. There are only thoughts, the experiences that linger. More pain than medicine can reach.

Today, the patient wakes as Sandy sits cross-legged in a chair, staring out at the courtyard during lunch. The patient says hello with timidity, he asks who is there, he asks, "Are you my granddaughter?" When Sandy stands, the patient asks, "Where are they?"

There are no clocks in this room, nothing to tick. Sandy is sure to be late to return. Walking over to the man who has skin like thin paper and eyes like milky glass is a journey in and of itself.

"Right here," Sandy says. Rattle repeats his daughter's name over and over. This, the same patient who insisted Sandy not call anyone, that there was no one to call.

Sandy wipes the man's head gently with a towel. "They're here," he repeats and presses two fingers into the patient's sternum, just firmly enough that he knows the impact will be felt. The patient's chest responds by expanding completely, if for an instant, before deflating. Sandy feels the man's shoulders soften, a predictable thing, as the pressure releases.

When the patient's last breath is fully released, there is the vague upturn of lips; Sandy glances at his smartwatch and types in the time. He eases the eyelids shut and looks back only once, glimpsing something like peace on the man's resting face, before shutting the door for the last time.

OUR SKY, THE OCEAN

We were waiting for rain the day my sister stopped talking. We stared upward, as a family, examining the swollen clouds, unsure. Mom and Dad prattled on about the football game that was holding up traffic to I-10, the church talent show, the neighbor's runaway Chihuahua, the taco stand opening up on Culebra, and the sad state of our garden.

Keeping an eye on my sister as she watered the vegetables, I chimed in from time to time. The broccoli and basil leaves were withered like prunes, and the lettuce resembled the tops of Grandpa's hands. Missy patted the ground and traced the leaves with her fingers like she was speaking to them without words.

"Do your job," I told the sky.

The twenty-day drought was right on schedule. It was the middle of August, and droughts hit the Texas Panhandle this time of year, every year. Still, no one was ever prepared.

Chuckling because our neighbor, Mr. Jerry, was bending over, I nudged my sister. It looked like he might lose his pants, and I whispered as much. When she smiled but didn't laugh, I began to worry.

I asked if she wanted to walk down to the Twenty & Below. We liked wandering the aisles to critique the new arrivals. We'd try on dresses and model for each other, spinning and sashaying and giggling until we were asked to kindly calm down or, if Darling was working, to kindly shut up.

"Come on," I coaxed. After a minute, I said, "Do you think it will rain?" When Missy didn't answer, I asked, "How much money do you think we'll earn if we help Mr. Jerry paint his garage next week?" I asked more questions, so many I don't remember.

Missy responded with raised eyebrows, half-smiles, shrugs, and bit lips. She walked with urgency, as though excited, but she didn't so much as peep. It was as if someone had pressed mute on some remote, the way my parents did during the commercials.

"You okay?" I asked.

She went slack jawed a moment. For dramatic effect, I guess, then smiled with a brightness I wasn't used to.

"Why aren't you talking?"

She examined me with her wide eyes. They were the same brown as our kitchen table, which Dad had stained extra dark; they had flecks of gold at the edges. I wished for her eyes. Mine were light blue like the sky on a day with no chance of rain.

We ran around the store and tried on clothes, but she was still hushed. Darling was working and said, "You girls are being so good today!" She gave us watermelon candies and instructed us to tuck them into our pockets for later.

My sister didn't appear ill. She ate her corn and mashed potatoes like a champ, even licking her plate clean, as the rest of us chattered on about this and that. Toward the end of the meal, Missy winked and gestured toward the door.

The air was pregnant with moisture. My parents were talking about who had bought the house at the end of the street and why the teenager three doors down had been fired from the automotive shop. They talked about the cell phone bill and what time they'd be home from work on Monday.

"Why aren't you saying anything?" I asked again.

A year ago, my sister closed her eyes and refused to look at anything for almost the entire day. She spent hours feeling around the house to get where she needed to go. After, when she finally opened them, she said that she was trying out a different way to see.

Missy slipped the candy in her mouth. She felt the dry earth around our vegetables.

"It's like sand," I said.

My sister sat down on a patch of dirt and began to carve a message with a small stick. "Try it," she wrote.

I traced my finger over the wrinkled lettuce and looked up at the sky. Together, we waited. At first, I could only hear my parents carrying on, but after a while I began to hear the wind, then the whoosh of cars nearby. I looked up at the sky and saw an ocean.

The first drop of rain hit my arm and made all the little hairs stand up. The next drop landed on my cheek with a splat. I leaned back and closed my eyes, absorbing each drop, as my sister's message melted into the mud.

ACKNOWLEDGMENTS

No creative work can find its way to completion without inspiration and support. I want to thank my family and friends. A very special thanks to Ashley Holloway, Stephanie Dickinson, Melissa Studdard, Jennifer Lynne Roberts, Joani Reese, Shannon Lakanen, Isabel Wolfe-Frischman, Marisela Chavez, Sandra Trevino, Beth Hoffman, and my B.M.W., Gretchen Phillips. These women inspire me by living courageously and creatively. Heartfelt gratitude to a phenomenal editor and supportive friend, Cindy Hochman.

Gratitude to the following publications, which published these stories, sometimes in slightly different form: "A Handbook for Single Mothers" in *Sunday Salon*, "Gather the Ingredients" in *Chicago Tribune's Printers Row*, "Don't Tease the Elephants" in *Monkeybicycle* and the limited print run of the chapbook, *Don't Tease the Elephants* (*Monkey Puzzle Press*), "Our Sky, the Ocean" in *Lunch Ticket*, "Green" in *Chicago Quarterly Review*, "The Couple on the Roof" in *Clackamas Literary Review*, "Emotional Intelligence" in *Cutthroat Magazine*, "Nebraska" as "The Migration" in *Midway Journal*, "Running Toward the Sun" in Fabula Press's *Aestas Anthology*, "Fortune in Smoke" in *Santa Fe Writers Project* (*SFWP Quarterly*), "The Glass City" in *Sequestrum*, "A Perpetual State of Awe" in *Atticus Review* and in slightly different form as "The Snowstorm" in *After the Gazebo*, "The Inconvenience of It All" in *The Saturday Evening Post*, "The Living Museum" in *Cleaver Magazine*, "The Shape of Loss" in *Change*

Seven Magazine, and "The Slope of a Line" in *Litbreak*.

ABOUT THE AUTHOR

Jen Knox (jenknox.com) earned her BA in English from Otterbein University and an MFA from Bennington College. She founded and co-runs Unleash Creatives, a holistic arts organization based in Reynoldsburg, Ohio. Jen works as a leadership program manager and lecturer at Ohio State University and teaches writing workshops. Her short fiction and creative nonfiction are taught in classrooms and appear in over a hundred publications around the world, including *The Best Small Fictions* (edited by Amy Hempel), *Chicago Tribune*, *Cutthroat Magazine*, *Chicago Quarterly Review*, *Room Magazine*, *Review Americana*, and *The Saturday Evening Post*. Her other collections include *After the Gazebo* (a Pen/Faulkner nominee) and *Resolutions*. She is the recipient of Prize Americana, the Montana Prize for Nonfiction from *CutBank*, and the Editor's Choice Award from *Flash Fiction Magazine*. *We Arrive Uninvited* was one of the top-rated projects of 2021 on *Coverfly's* Red List for family stories, won the Steel Toe Books (STB) Award in Prose, and was released in March 2023.

39952956R00118